RED HOT RANCHER

PART-TIME COWBOYS, BOOK 2

MARIE JOHNSTON

LE PUBLISHING

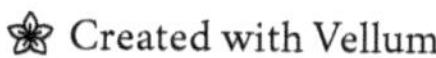 Created with Vellum

Full-time fireman and part-time rancher Caleb is living the bachelor's dream and staying rent-free in his best friend's place. Too bad it's because he lost his house to a tornado and his best friend's sister is the one that got away. At least she doesn't visit often—the last thing he needs is to show her she was right about him: he's going nowhere fast. But when her cheating fiancé kicks her out, she has no place to go except her brother's suddenly too-crowded ranch house.

After a streak of bad decisions, Brigit has to slink back home to nurse her wounds and find a job. To complete her humiliation, there's no way she can avoid the first love she walked away from years ago—because he's sleeping on the other side of her wall. At least it's only a matter of time before she's gone again. After all, there's nothing in this town for her but bullies and cow patties…except a fireman in cowboy boots who melts her heart and makes her consider love again.

He's not leaving. She's not staying. If the reason they can't be together is so simple, why is it so hard to remember?

For my mom-friends raising kids with RAD.

CHAPTER 1

Brigit scowled at her laptop. The coffee shop was empty except for her and two elderly men lamenting the state of soybeans. It was all she could do not to add her two cents, but picturing their reaction was enough to stop her. She'd be surprised, even a little relieved, if they argued with her, but most likely she'd get a "that's nice, honey" or some chuckles about why a young girl like herself would be interested in market prices.

Why buy that attitude here when she could go home and get it for free?

With an indignant sniff, she focused on the screen and the dismal list of job openings in the surrounding area. Her fiancé Oliver wouldn't move for a position less than CEO. The trouble was that she didn't have the experience. Neither did he, which was why he'd decided to move back to their hometown of Moore, leaving her no choice but to go with.

Which was why she was sitting in a café in Normandy over an hour away from Moore. No witnesses to see her struggling to find work. The mighty Brigit Walker had slunk back to Moore because she couldn't hack it in the big wide world.

Maybe she shouldn't have been so cocky as a teen, informing everyone who would listen that she was going to Do Something with her life and Go Somewhere and be a Big Deal.

The final joke was on her. Her shiny new MBA didn't mean much when she couldn't get a job that'd cover both a mortgage and a car payment.

Good thing Oliver was taking such good care of her.

She checked her watch. He'd take his lunch hour soon and she could surprise him with an iced coffee—real cream, please—and discuss the locations of some of these positions. A few were within commuting distance, but any driving in the middle of a Minnesota winter made commuting a major consideration, and Oliver was already driving an hour for his work.

It was early November and they had yet to see flurries, but her stomach was already churning at the thought of him driving on icy roads. But he'd insisted on renting a house in Moore, and then on staying there when she commented on their lease being up for renewal soon. It would have been a good time to get out.

Don't worry, Brigit. I'm doing the driving and paying the rent. There are no places this nice in Normandy. Just stay in Moore and look for a job. Maybe something online?

She took a sip of her nonfat iced caramel macchiato. The sweet, cool drink washed over her tongue, putting a damper on her bitterness. Oliver managed to point out that he covered the bills in nearly every conversation. Just like her mom managed to comment on her lack of interest in pursuing med school.

The twinkle of her three-quarter-carat diamond ring caught her eye. She stretched out her hand. The light bouncing off the diamond made sparkles dance on her finger. She glanced around to make sure no one had caught her preening over her own ring. The soybean guys had just walked out. She craned her neck to peek beyond the partition she'd stuffed herself behind. The barista was busy at a counter with her back to the booths.

Okay, the coast was clear. She stared at her ring again. Each time she looked at it, the clarity of the jewel stole her breath. Then anxiety squeezed her chest. What if she lost it? What if she banged it too hard against the grain truck when she was climbing in and the stone fell out? Oliver would be so pissed and not only because she'd lost an expensive stone that he'd bought, but also because she'd been "playing farm girl" again.

She clenched her fist.

That was half her motivation to find a high-paying job right there. Financial freedom. Mom had paid for her undergraduate and graduate school tuition. Oliver had paid the rest of her expenses while she took her classes, so she hadn't needed to maintain a job on top of school.

The door squeaked open, but Brigit refrained from being a small-town gawker. She kept her head down and scooted closer to the partition that separated her from the counter. Just in case anyone recognized her. She hadn't met many people since Oliver started working in Normandy, but residents of Moore did come to here occasionally. She didn't want to answer the dreaded "oh, what are you doing here" question that was loaded with the "don't you have a job" insinuations or the "life without Mommy and Daddy's help wasn't as easy as you thought it would be" gloat.

Maybe all that was in her imagination, but she heard the unspoken words so much clearer.

A breathy voiced drifted over the partition. "Ooh, that looks so yummy."

The woman must be commenting on the pumpkin spice latte placard by the cash register. Brigit was tempted to peek, but with the way she'd have to stretch, she'd look ridiculous if she got busted.

Besides, a woman with that rich, sexy voice probably didn't have to worry about the calorie bomb lurking in the drink. Brigit's hips liked lattes a little too much. Oliver had noticed her weight increase since they'd moved back home.

Yoga's great for your ass. Aren't you going anymore?

"You gonna get that?" a familiar voice asked. "You know I'm buying."

Wait… That throaty rumble, the way it dripped with innuendo… She blinked and cocked her head. No, she must've heard wrong.

The barista greeted them and rattled off the daily specials. The breathy woman ordered her venti PSL and the man ordered an iced coffee. "With real cream, please."

Brigit frowned. No, she wasn't imagining it. She knew that voice.

What were the odds? Should she pop up and say "hey"—

Breathy woman giggled and murmured something under her breath. They couldn't see her, and she couldn't see them or hear the whispers they volleyed at each other, but their intimate tones were unmistakable. Brigit's stomach twisted.

These two were more than friends.

"I probably shouldn't have ordered that drink," breathy woman murmured. "Not with all the Halloween candy still at work."

"Don't worry," Oliver replied. "I'll work it off you later."

Breathy woman tittered again. "This time, let's make it past my foyer."

"I can't help myself around you."

A tiny smack of lips carried over the wall. Were they kissing? Stomach acid clawed up her throat and she hunched lower.

Faint laughs and suggestive murmurs continued until the barista said, "Here ya go. Thanks for stopping in."

Footsteps faded and then the door opened and closed. Brigit let out a slow exhale and stared at the now-black screen in front of her. What should she do? Right now, her heart pounded but her feet were as heavy as salt blocks.

The barista came around the partition with a cloth in her hand. "Still doing okay?"

No. Brigit nodded.

The other girl let out a wistful sigh. "I just love seeing couples so into each other. And when the man dotes on his woman like that…" The lady fanned herself.

Brigit clenched her jaw and released it. She smacked the lid of the laptop down, her ring catching the light, only now its sparkle made her numb. "She's not his woman."

I am.

IT WAS MOVING DAY. After an ugly confrontation with Oliver, Brigit was packed and ready to leave. Because she'd been kicked out.

Could the humiliation be any worse?

She stared at her oblivious brother. He'd been the first person she'd turned to, and like always, her twin was here to rescue her. Justin stood in the doorway, but he wasn't the problem. The guy he'd brought to help her move was the issue. She trained her gaze over Justin's shoulder to where his red pickup was lined along the curb for easy loading.

Caleb Cruise was opening the horse trailer doors and digging out blankets for her furniture. The long-sleeved button-up shirt couldn't hide the bunching of muscles on his lean frame. And the way it was tucked into his jeans gave her a grade A view of his ass as he set his toolbox on the lawn.

Caleb Cruise. The man she'd tried to avoid her entire adult life.

And he was here to help her move out of the home she'd shared with her cheating ex-fiancé.

She'd rather get her foot stomped on by a half-ton heifer.

Caleb looked up as he straightened. His face didn't break into a smile. He gave her a nod, like he always had the few times their paths had crossed in the last decade. Thankfully, he didn't wait for a response. She wasn't prepared to deal with Caleb or the unresolved feelings between them that she'd ignored since she'd left.

Forget the feelings. She wasn't equipped to be seen by anyone outside her family. This morning, she'd rolled out of bed after a night full of tears and tissues and dressed in the yoga pants that, according to Oliver, made her ass look big. She'd topped the look with a messy topknot and an old pink T-shirt that had a hole under the armpit.

Moving was hard work, but Caleb looked like he'd be going to a photo shoot afterward. He always did, no matter how he was dressed. When he was on for his twenty-four-hour shift with the fire department, he was Caleb the firefighter. Navy-blue uniform, his hair slicked back revealing his shaved sides. No ear gauges or nose ring.

But off duty, he was a mixture of ranch kid and alt rocker. A combo that shouldn't work, but with Caleb, it couldn't have worked better. Today he had a ball cap over his glossy hair, but his ear gauges were in. The ear gear wasn't large enough to make his earlobes saggy when the plugs were out, and they paired well with his nose ring. In high school, he'd had an eyebrow piercing and a tongue ring, too, but with his work, he'd let those go.

Not that she'd noticed.

"I don't have much stuff, Justin," she said tightly. "You and I could have handled it."

It would've taken all day, and maybe some of the furniture would've broken their backs, but she and Justin were enough.

Justin snorted and pushed past her. "Sorry, I want to walk in the morning and I know that china hutch is gonna make me its bitch. Besides, you didn't want to make a big deal out of it and Caleb was around when you called." Justin wandered through the living room, pointing at the large furniture and muttering to himself.

He was making a game plan to load everything in as few trips as possible. At least one of them had the wherewithal to do it. When she considered all the work that needed to be done, she broke down in tears, all the ways her life had gone wrong rolling like a sad black-and-white movie through her mind.

When she'd called Justin five days ago, she'd been sobbing and shaking in her car in the parking lot of the coffee shop in Normandy. Before she'd confronted Oliver, she'd called her brother. All her college friends had graduated and moved on. They were immersed in exciting careers and a few were married and starting families. There was no way Brigit was going to call and tell them the story of how the barista thought her fiancé and the coworker he was fucking were such an adorable couple.

Would she have called Justin, knowing Caleb was standing next to him? Justin had waited to point it out until last night when she'd contacted him in a moment of panic.

Oliver had moved his things out when she couldn't accept his indiscretion as a mistake—or take full blame because the stress of supporting her had driven him into his coworker's arms.

Apparently, he'd been a busy boy, because yesterday he'd

called with the news that he'd cut ties with the rental house. All the papers were in his name and she needed to leave. Now.

Oh, and Vanessa and I will stop by and get the car. Leave the keys in the mailbox.

Brigit's car was also in his name. That had been the deal. He had a good job and had secured the financing and she'd bought the furniture with her parents' help. The engagement ring went with him as well, as if he'd sensed she would've been first in line at Moore's pawnshop the next day. She should've done that immediately. Then maybe she could've skipped him blaming her for yet another issue between them.

This won't even cover everything I've done to get you through school.

Guess the ring wasn't a symbol of his deep, abiding love for her after all.

So, he'd dissolved the rental agreement and was selling her car. It was like he was punishing her for outing his affair.

She turned to see what Caleb was doing, still lost as to what she should pitch in with. Her pulse jumped. He was swaggering up the walk, the brim of his hat shading his eyes. She abruptly spun away from the door.

Yes, it was pretty fucking rude. He was using his day off to help her, but there was only so much emotional turmoil a girl could take. She'd have to give him a cold shoulder or she'd be hiding in the bathroom for half the day.

"Hey, Bridge." God, that voice. Deeper than Oliver's, but always with a ray of positivity. Caleb was an eternal optimist, and she hadn't met anyone that made her laugh more since they'd broken up. "Hope you don't mind that I invited myself along to help."

"It's your back." She tried not looking at him but failed. His mouth tightened but not with irritation at her. Sympathy brimmed in his warm brown eyes. Her commitment to aloof bitchiness wavered. "But thanks. You didn't have to."

"You shouldn't have had to find a new home on such short notice."

She smiled sadly, the last of her intentions to stay icy melting away. "You had to with even less notice."

He grimaced at the reminder of the tornado that had destroyed his house a few months ago. "Both shitty events. Good thing we have Justin to crash with."

Her lungs seized. In her mental state, she hadn't put the two together. Justin was coming to grab her things and store them in the shop at his place. And while she knew Caleb was staying with Justin until he could finance the build of a new house, she hadn't paired that information with the fact that she'd be moving in with Justin until she found a job.

She'd be living under the same roof as the one man she'd been avoiding.

A shadow crossed Caleb's face. "Don't worry. The house is big enough that I won't bother you." He stalked past her, his jaw tight.

She scrubbed her face with her hands. Had she looked that upset at the prospect? She was, but she hadn't meant to hurt his feelings, and not just because he planned to haul all her quality-built furniture.

He'd lost his grandmother's hundred-year-old house in a tornado. He literally had no home, but he still had a ranch to run and a full-time job. She had poor taste in men and had stupidly given Oliver too much control over their finances. The only smart thing she'd done was go to that coffee shop and eavesdrop on him. Otherwise, this might have been her life, only getting divorced with nothing to her name but a china hutch she'd never wanted to buy.

But it's a statement piece. Mom had loved it and she'd been buying, so Brigit had acquiesced.

The guys disappeared into her bedroom. A flush ran up her neck to her cheeks. Caleb was in her bedroom again, only under tragically different circumstances. At least she'd gotten up early and stripped the bedding, tossing the mattress cover. She was keeping the bed—she wasn't trashing a pillow-top king-sized bed just because Oliver was a douche.

Her eyes burned with the threat of tears as she scanned her furniture. A living room set, dining room set, bedroom set, artwork, decor. All of it sturdy, none of it made from particleboard. Each piece was large and heavy. Good thing the house was old and small and she hadn't furnished the basement.

Her shoulders sagged as a wave of fatigue washed over her. Between all the crying and the late-night packing, exhaustion was her best friend. How convenient that spot was open, since she'd been glued to Oliver's damn side for the last three years. She no longer had a bestie.

And that was the real reason she hadn't had anyone to call but Justin. She was alone, except for her two new roommates: her brother—and the ex-boyfriend no one knew she'd ever dated.

CHAPTER 2

*C*aleb set the painting on the top of his boot and watched Brigit hip-check a dresser into place between the box springs and mattress. He hadn't seen her dressed so casually in years. Not since the days he'd hung out with Justin on his farm, when she'd be out on the riding lawn mower, her hair in the messy bun at the top of her head. Then, he'd had such a huge fucking crush on her. She'd been the cutest girl alive.

She'd gone from cute to sexy. Her curves had filled out, making his mouth water at the woman she'd become. For a while he'd wondered if she'd grow taller than him. But she'd stopped before reaching six feet, and he'd managed to squeak past.

It didn't matter, their height. At one time, they'd fit perfectly together. Until he'd endured a teenage boy's worst nightmare—being busted by her mother.

You will get dressed and you will leave and you will forget you know my daughter's name. None of the fires he'd been in scared him as much as Joan Walker's voice undulating with rage.

He'd been allowed to stay friends with Justin and that was only because it would've attracted attention otherwise. Justin might've known Caleb was hot for his sister, but he didn't know that he and Brigit had crossed any lines. Or that he'd snuck into her room and out to meet her in the fields all summer to make out and experiment the way kids that age do.

She brushed a few strands of stray blond hair out of her face, shaking him out of the past and into the present. While she looked sexier than ever, she still had dark crescents under her eyes and a perpetual frown.

For today, he allowed himself to absolve himself of the anger and hurt he'd been harboring since that fateful night she'd ghosted him. He'd had plenty of time to come to terms with his decision last night, when he and Justin had spent three hours hosing down and washing the horse trailer so her furniture wouldn't get horse shit all over it and smell like manure.

He didn't miss her sigh as she hopped down to the concrete.

"You've been hauling all morning," he said. "Why don't you take a breather?"

She arched a light brow. "Are you going to sit and rest?"

The corner of his mouth hitched. Always with the attitude. But usually only toward him. He'd noticed the difference as a kid. Toward her parents, teachers, and classmates, she was Perfect Brigit. To him—Sassy Brigit. He used to think that meant he was special, but no. The night he'd had his ever-loving mind blown, she must not have felt the same. Her mom had caught them together and Brigit had been done with him. Just like that.

Ancient history, and memories like that had no business surfacing on a day like today. She was hurting and pale and as homeless as he was. Maybe a little less, since Justin's house was the home she'd grown up in.

The place Caleb had spent most of his childhood in was in a landfill. He was trying to rebuild, but the insurance payout was dismal, and building a house out of town in Moore, Minnesota, was more expensive than he'd thought. He choked back the stress that threatened to rise. He had his ranch, and his buddy Jesse was helping with the cattle.

But the weight of not having an address to call his own descended on him at random moments. Like now, standing outside of a white horse trailer with a mass-produced picture of a fake seaside resting on his boot.

This picture had Joan Walker all over it. He might not have had much to do with Brigit since he was eighteen, but not once had she dreamed about beaches or lighthouses. Blooming alfalfa pastures and pole barns, maybe.

"Here." He handed Brigit the frame. The whole package only weighed ten pounds and the blanket he'd wrapped it in was less than two pounds. She looked so damn exhausted, he didn't want her carting another nightstand out on her back.

She took it without argument, proving just how tired she was.

He went back inside. Justin was dragging out boxes from the bedroom and dumping them on the living room floor.

"I want to see it all together," Justin said. "I want to get every-thing in one trip so we don't have to leave Bridge here alone."

"In case Assface comes back." He'd never liked Oliver. The guy hadn't passed up a single opportunity to insinuate that Caleb was a loser for staying in Moore. Then Oliver had moved back, acting like a worldly scholar—one who needed his dad to get him a job.

Justin sneered, his blue eyes flashing. "Bastard won't get another chance to make her feel like shit."

Caleb had his issues with Brigit, but Oliver was a controlling, insecure idiot. "And she can't drive away if he shows."

Justin nodded. "I wouldn't put it past him to watch and lock us out before we can get the rest."

"Yeah, given the power play he pulled with her yesterday." Last night, Brigit's sobs resonating from Justin's phone had made Caleb nearly homicidal. Suddenly, he hadn't cared one bit how she'd ignored him; he'd only wanted to rush to her side and comfort her. He'd practically begged to help today.

"You can always take the truck and unload it with her," Justin said. "I can wait here. The jackass won't try anything with me."

"That'll work." Brigit might have something to say about being alone with him, but her ex would give Caleb more trouble than Justin. He glanced at all the items yet to load. "Is all this going with us?"

"He only paid for what gave him control." Justin's expression darkened. "He guilted Brigit into paying for the rest. She worked for me and did online tutoring. Mom and Dad helped her with the rest."

How had Brigit missed what Oliver was like? Or hadn't she wanted to know?

Caleb carried the dresser drawers from the bedroom to the living room. The plan was to pack the large items into the trailer and use the smaller stuff like boxes and drawers to fill in the empty spaces between. He dropped his load and ignored the scrappy lace spilling out of it. He had enough Brigit fantasies haunting his life. His adult mind had filled them in with richer details as he'd gotten older. The confirmation wouldn't help him sleep at night. Because he wasn't rubbing one off in the borrowed childhood bedroom of his friend while a despondent Brigit lay next door in her old room.

His claim that they wouldn't have to cross paths wasn't

necessarily true. Justin slept in the master bedroom his brother Travis had vacated when he'd built his own house. The room Caleb was using and the one Brigit was staying in were upstairs. And there was only one bathroom on that level, so…

But he was gone twenty-four hours at a time, so he'd only be tortured during his days off.

The door banged open and Justin jingled the keys. "She's already in the truck."

Caleb grabbed the keys and went out. When he climbed into the F-250, Brigit was in the passenger seat with her arms folded, but her standard cool look was gone. Her head rested against the window and she curled into the door as much as her seat belt would allow.

He didn't know what to say, so he started the engine.

"I bet they're all wondering what's going on." Her voice was small as her gaze touched on each house in the neighborhood.

Caleb followed her gaze. The houses were quiet. No one peered out any window, and there hadn't been much traffic. From the horse trailer full of furniture, it'd be clear Brigit and Oliver were moving out. It might even be obvious they weren't moving out together.

"It wasn't your fault." Those words felt both stupid and necessary.

"His cheating wasn't my fault. But I should've seen how dismissive and manipulative he is." She paused. "He's subtle though. Not that it would've made a difference if he weren't."

"Have you told your parents yet?" Joan and Rick Walker lived in Arizona. Joan would outrun cops to be by Brigit's side.

"Nope. Mom really liked Oliver." Was that why she hadn't called her mother yet? Afraid Joan would tell her she should've stuck it out and worked on the relationship?

They wound through town and hit the highway that would take them to Justin's. They'd have to pass all her cousins' houses on the way when they turned off the highway. She'd asked Justin not to mention anything to them. Apparently the thought of a family swarm of support and comfort frightened her. Was it because that would call attention to her ordeal? He didn't know, but all the Walkers would find out eventually. Oliver was smart to move out of Moore as soon as possible.

At Justin's place, he backed the trailer up to the shop entrance. Brigit hopped out and opened the large sliding door. Together, they offloaded all the items without talking more than was needed to give directions and figure out where to place stuff.

He tried to ignore how much he enjoyed being around her. She wasn't outright ignoring him, or giving him the stiff nod she used in public to keep people from asking why she wasn't giving her brother's good friend the time of day. Every time she walked by, he caught a whiff of her lotion, or shampoo, or whatever lightly scented product she used. He'd lived too long by himself if it was a thrill to smell a girl.

But Brigit wasn't a girl anymore and he was reminded of that each time she bent over to pick up a box. The way her stretchy pants caressed her ass filled him with jealousy. She'd finally allowed herself some dessert and wasn't all angles and bones. Of course she'd looked good then, too, but this seemed more…natural. More like the girl who used to sprint through the pastures and swing herself up onto a horse bareback. More like a woman who was comfortable in her own skin. A sexy woman he wanted to touch. A lot.

She wiped her forearm across her face, smearing dust and grit. The temp hovered above freezing, but they'd worked up a sweat. "That didn't take nearly as long as I thought."

"Unloading never does."

Her face clouded over as she took in the pile of her belongings. "I can't believe my whole life fits into a corner of the shop." Before he could reply, she spun and marched out. "I wish I had time to cuddle some lambs, but I guess I'll be doing that every morning now."

He trotted out behind her and closed up the shop. Tomorrow, he and Justin would arrange the furniture on pallets and cover them with sheets. They'd already put out extra mousetraps. Wherever Brigit was going next, she didn't need critters popping out of her couch.

"Justin won't put you to work." He went around to the passenger side where Brigit's fine behind was sticking out of the door. He bit back his groan. She was wiggling as she wrestled her duffel bag out.

"I got the rest," he offered.

She hesitated. *Please don't turn me down.* He couldn't walk away and leave her to drag her luggage to the house, but she'd know he was eying her body if he suddenly turned and stared at the fields behind the shop.

She stepped back, the bag slung over her shoulder and her arms full of pillows. He reached in to grab her suitcase and her blankets. A backpack was sitting on the seat and he slung that over his shoulder. A hard thump hit his ribs and he grunted.

His long strides caught up with her. "This backpack would make a good weapon."

"Oh, those are my old textbooks. Too bad keeping them doesn't guarantee my ability to get a job."

Justin had joked that Brigit was a professional student. "Look, Bridge. You have time. Justin isn't forcing you to go anywhere. He won't care if you pitch in around here or work in town."

"I'm *not* staying in Moore," she muttered as she wrestled her gear through the side door of the house.

Tell me how you really feel. He'd never understood why she was adamant about leaving town to create a life. But then she'd never experienced a transient lifestyle like he had.

Caleb followed her inside. The house was newer than his grandma's had been, though it had the same two-story farmhouse look and was easily twice as large. The kitchen was spacious and separate from the dining room. A den and the master bedroom were on the first floor. The stairs creaked as they went up to the second floor, where there were three bedrooms and a full-sized bath. His boots pounded ominously on the hardwood.

If Caleb could design his own place, he'd build a knock-off of a farmhouse like this. He might not be able to afford the same square footage, but he hoped he could get more than a manufactured home on pillars.

He wanted a home of his own. People wondered why he'd moved into Grandma's dilapidated home after she died, but they didn't understand. That place had been the only home he'd known, the only one where he'd been welcome. Her house had been a castle to him. And unlike his mom, Grandma had always been around.

Some people questioned why he ranched when he was only a one-man operation and had a full-time job, but that ranch had been in his family for generations. Perhaps people assumed that since his mom had been adopted, the place didn't mean as much to him.

Brigit charged into her room. He cautiously followed her, plagued by the apprehension he'd experienced as a kid. From when they were little and she'd screamed at him and Justin to stay out, or later, when they'd discovered a mutual attraction and hadn't wanted to get caught. That fear had propelled them to hook up in the great outdoors.

She dumped her load on the bed. The space was as plain as a hotel room. Her personality had been stripped from it, perhaps from when her other brother Travis had owned the place. The bedding was beige with a brick design and the walls were bare. The off-white carpet was the same, but nearly pristine. She must not have been allowed to even have water up here.

Caleb made sure to eat in the kitchen, and except for today, he always took his boots off when he came through the door. It might be Justin's house, but after years of getting the stink eye from Joan, he didn't want to risk her wrath.

"I guess we'd better get back." She wasn't looking at him, and her arms were hugged around herself.

The years bled away until it was just him and his old friend Brigit. Forget the abandonment, the lack of faith, and the hurt between them. They'd been friends once.

"Hey," he said softly and crept around to get a look at her face. Her eyes were squeezed shut as she pressed her lips together. He didn't care what their history was or why she'd wanted nothing to do with him since their night together, he wanted to comfort her.

She dropped her face into her hands. He wrapped his arms around her and held her while her shoulders shook.

Oliver needed his ass kicked. Brigit—the real Brigit—went to the ends of the earth for the ones she loved. There was nothing she wouldn't do. This Brigit, the put-together ice princess other people saw, was melting in his arms. When this moment ended, which Brigit would she be?

CHAPTER 3

This was her happy place.

Around her, small wooly sheep roamed, an occasional bleat bouncing off the barn walls. She'd always loved working with animals, and sheep ranching was a recent addition to the family business. Each time she was home, she learned something new. So she tried to help as much as she could, like checking hooves for hoof rot before the snow started to fly.

And it took her mind off living with Caleb.

That was a lie.

Being in his arms again had dusted off those old emotions she'd refused to analyze, the part of her brain that thought he'd hung the moon and aligned the stars just for her. Or noticed they fit together better than they had when they were teenagers.

She was only a couple of inches shorter than him. She was probably three milkshakes past doing the boyfriend jeans thing with his pants. But when he held her...she'd never felt so feminine, so petite. None of her boyfriends after

Caleb, and certainly not Oliver, had ever made her feel that way, and there were times she craved it.

"Come on," she cooed to the ewes as she released them back into the pasture.

She missed working cattle, but sheep had their own brand of easy. By herself, she could muscle an ewe around, even a ram, and perform several duties on her own if Justin was busy. Working cattle was a team effort, and that carried its own thrill, but this? This was a nice change from living in Minneapolis. No traffic. No driving to a park just to be outside. While there was plenty to do on a ranch, the pace was slower. It had changed her twin. Justin didn't act like the uptight prick he'd been when he'd lived in Denver.

Seeing him joking around with Caleb was a blast from the past that only tumbled all those pesky memories to the top of her brain.

Today, Caleb was gone, working his twenty-four. She'd get a small reprieve from the stress of running into him. This morning, she'd snuck out of her room to use the bathroom just as Caleb had been coming out. She had rubbed her eyes and pretended to be groggy when she'd actually been stunned into silence at the sight of his wide shoulders and his navy-blue uniform top. His hair had been slicked back and to the side in a dapper but edgy way. And the way his pants had tapered over his strong thighs… It was just too much for a girl to take that early in the morning. He'd given her a curt "morning" and swaggered down the stairs. She'd stood frozen for a few heartbeats before realizing that she'd forgotten what she'd gotten out of bed to do.

Justin was wandering through the barn, his ball cap pulled down low and his boots crunching in the straw. The noise popped her fireman-Caleb fantasy.

"You didn't do all my work for me already, did you?" He scanned the dim interior of the structure. The doors on both ends of the barn were open, if only partway, letting in the daylight.

"I listed the ones I inspected in the record book." Brigit shoved her hands into her jeans pockets. "I suppose I should go inside and do more job hunting or I'll be underfoot."

"Any ideas where you're going to look? Or are you going to try for law school again?"

She averted her gaze and repressed a shudder. Law school hadn't been her dream, just an idea Mom had thrown around that gained more traction than Brigit ever planned. "No, I don't think it's for me."

"I'm not surprised. If you said you wanted to go to vet school, maybe, but I couldn't see you being a lawyer."

She swatted him. "What are you saying? That I'm better with animals than people?"

He cocked his head and shot her a knowing look.

Laughter bubbled out of her. "Right. And no to vet school. I'd rather work with the outsides of animals, not dig around their insides."

"So then where are you applying? I know you're not staying in Moore."

Swallowing around the small lump in her throat, she grappled for an answer. Why was it hard to toss out a city? It couldn't be leaving Moore that was bothering her—just homesickness. She was back home, but it wasn't her home. It was Justin's.

"Probably Minneapolis." She'd lived there since leaving home after graduation. The city was…not home. Familiar. "I should get back inside. And call Mom." That was one more task she had to do, and she'd sworn not to put it off any longer. She hadn't planned to mention anything, but Justin would understand.

His expression changed from reassuring to sympathetic,

and compassion simmered in his blue eyes. "You're doing the deed, huh?"

"I'm surprised she hasn't tracked me down already."

"Being in Arizona delays the grapevine."

"Well it's been almost five days now. I'm still in the small window of forgiveness for leaving her out. Wish me luck."

Brigit trudged through the barn and out into the sunshine. A fall breeze cool with the frigid promise of snow blew across her, but the effect was lessened by the warm rays beating down on her. Birds chirped around the house as they hunted for late fall fare. The bleats of the sheep faded behind her.

Calling her own mother shouldn't feel like this much of a chore, but Mom had adored Oliver. The woman hadn't said as much, but Brigit knew without asking that she'd had fantasies of her daughter being married to a successful businessman, and even better, one who had a last name almost as respected in the town of Moore as Walker.

Inside, Brigit kicked her boots off by the door and jogged up to her room to grab her phone. There were no messages, no "I miss you" texts from her ex, and no cheer-up comments from all the friends she didn't have. Her social circle had consisted of Oliver's friends, and she supposed it was like a divorce. He got all the people, she got all the loneliness.

If she thought about the phone call too hard, it wouldn't happen. She punched in her mom's number and waited for her to pick up.

"Hey, I was just thinking about you." At the sound of Mom's cheerful voice, Brigit sank onto her bed and rested her head in her hand.

Skipping the greeting, she went straight for the gut. "Oliver and I broke up. He was cheating on me."

"Oh, honey." Mom paused. Her breath echoed over the

line, like she was opening her mouth to say something and closing it again. "Who? How? Why…"

The story spilled out of Brigit, every humiliating detail. She didn't spare one moment of the coffee-shop debacle, hoping that would sway her mom's opinion of what Brigit should have done.

"I just can't believe it." Mom's exasperated huff sounded angry. That was a promising sign. "Wasn't he willing to work out any issues?"

"What was there to work out? We were barely engaged and he was already sleeping with someone else."

"It's not your fault he turned to another. Did he say at all why he did it?"

There could be so many reasons. He felt like he was carrying her through life? She wasn't good enough in bed? He didn't like the way she looked anymore? It all added up to him being unhappy with her.

"We didn't get that far in our conversation." She'd been unwilling to hear how she "made" him do it.

"And you weren't interested in repairing the relationship?"

"No, Mom. I figured that if he couldn't keep it in his pants even with a ring on my finger, he wasn't worth one more minute of sharing my life." Brigit pressed her lips shut. She never lashed out at Mom. Not after all the woman had done for her. "I want a rock-solid foundation before I get married, not a wing and a prayer."

The hard edge of her voice kept Mom from replying right away. "You deserve nothing less. I just thought—the way you talked about him… I'm surprised you're letting him go. So what now?"

The way she talked about him? Brigit thought back. No, she never had discussed those times Oliver made her feel less than, or the belittling comments he made. She hadn't wanted to hear anyone else agree. "Well, since I was kicked out of the house, Justin helped me move. I'm staying with him." She held her breath, waiting for the news to sink in.

"Isn't… Isn't Caleb staying with Justin?" There it was. The other major reason she'd put off this phone call. Mom would breathe easier if Brigit didn't share the same roof as Caleb, or better yet if Caleb moved to a different country, maybe the one his mom had been born in.

"Yeah, he's here too. But he works one full day, and his days off he spends working on his own ranch." She should leave it at that, but more explanation might help Mom accept her new living arrangements. Being roommates with him wasn't going to anchor her to Moore and make her give up all that schooling Mom had fought for. "You remember his house was destroyed by a tornado?"

Mom snorted. "No surprise. It was probably only a couple steps away from being condemned."

No, it hadn't been. Caleb's grandparents might not have had enough money to update the look of the house in the last several decades, but she'd cared for what she had. Including Caleb.

"Either way, he lost his home. And I lost my home. Thankfully, Justin is still single, and we can both crash with him."

"Crashing with him is one thing but living with him is another. I know you'll help your brother out. Has Caleb paid him even one penny in rent?"

"He's trying to rebuild his house, Mom. I got kicked out by a selfish prick. Caleb's trying to rebuild his life and his best friend is helping him. You know Justin isn't the type to let people use him."

"You've always had a blind spot when it comes to that boy."

"And you've always had a lot of judgment when it comes

to him." Brigit pressed her lips together and squeezed her eyes shut. If it weren't for Mom, things between her and Caleb might have turned out so differently. But ultimately, it'd been her decision to cut things off and leave town.

She couldn't dwell on the past. Good, bad, or indifferent, it didn't change that Mom had once asked Brigit if she was willing to give up school and a career to be stuck in Moore. She'd had one shot at school, and Mom had fought for it.

I finally got your father to agree to pay for your school, wherever you choose, instead of doing exactly what you're doing now—settling for the first boy that makes your heart go pitter-patter.

Caleb did more than that, but Mom had been right. Her parents had put Travis through school. Justin had big plans. But when it came to Brigit, Dad looked at all his sisters-in-law who'd settled down with ranchers and wondered why she couldn't do the same and save him the money.

"Brigit. It was for the best." So much emotion saturated Mom's words. Was she not proud of the way she'd divided her and Caleb as kids?

Shame elbowed out her anger. Those years in high school when Brigit had been looking at colleges was the only time she'd heard actual shouting between her parents.

Don't you dare make my decision to marry you and give up my own life goals Brigit's curse, Rick.

It doesn't have to do with you or me, Joan. It has to do with our future, our retirement.

Our kids are our future.

"I'm sorry. I didn't mean to bring that up." And look how it had turned out. Had Dad been right? "But I feel like you think I should've tried to patch things up with Oliver and settle." Which was what she'd fought against all those years ago.

"You're right, you're right. He was such a promising young man, and you spoke so highly of him."

No, she'd just skipped the snide comments and his controlling ways. As if not speaking about them made his behavior less real. "The last few days haven't been easy." Tears burned the backs of her eyes. "I guess I have to figure out what I want to be when I grow up."

"Don't you still want to be a lawyer?"

I never wanted to be a lawyer. "I have to be realistic. I'm not getting any younger, and I can't live with Justin for the rest of my life."

"No, Moore isn't the place for you. You have too much potential to let it go to waste in a small town like that."

Like you did, Mom? Mom had been the college girl with all life had to offer in front of her when she'd met Dad. But Dad had gone to college only so he could come back home and run the farm and ranch with his brothers. It was either give Dad up or give her dreams up, and Mom probably hadn't thought her dreams were gone for good when she moved to Moore. But then she'd stayed home, had babies, and hadn't touched anything relevant to her college career since.

Farm wife were like two four-letter curse words when it came to Mom, and she'd drilled into Brigit all her life not to throw it all away for a boy.

As Mom started on her laundry list of Things Brigit is Destined for in Life, Brigit sprawled backward on the bed. She'd ridden out this conversation before. Only this time, she couldn't help but wonder just how much good following Mom's path was doing her.

CHAPTER 4

ith his shift over, Caleb had to change before he could check on his place. He jogged up the stairs to Justin's front door and gripped the doorknob. First, he had to steel himself. He had two days off. Two days to avoid Brigit.

He never thought he'd reach a point in his life where one full day lost to the firehouse was something he looked forward to. Battling fires was one thing; hanging around a bunch of guys doing menial tasks was another.

Okay, he could do this. She might not even be home. Not like it mattered.

Her scent surrounded him at the most unexpected times. The bathroom had become a torture chamber. Her shampoo sat next to his on the bathtub ledge, her toothbrush and toothpaste were only inches away from his own, and that lotion she spread on every night was like a field full of wildflowers blossoming inside his head.

And that was just her presence. Seeing her was even harder.

Cold leeched through his uniform. He twisted the knob and stepped inside.

Damn, he had shitty timing.

She was standing in the middle of the living room pulling her long blond hair up into a ponytail that would fit out of the back of her ball cap. It would be too awkward to back out of the house now. He had no choice but to move forward.

She peered under her raised arm. "Morning."

"Morning." It was the same word he'd said yesterday coming out of the bathroom. She'd been adorable, squinting in the light and frowning at him. He hadn't wanted to leave, could've soaked in the sight of her in pajama pants and a T-shirt for months, but he'd convinced himself to keep moving.

He was staring at her now. They looked at each other for a couple of seconds, like neither one of them knew what else to do. It was Justin's place, but his friend was never around when Caleb needed him to run interference. But then Justin had no clue what had transpired between himself and Brigit, or that she was why he was approaching thirty with no history of long-term relationships.

"Have you eaten breakfast?" He might as well make himself useful. Breakfast was usually on his own, while his other meals were eaten at the firehouse. Part of contributing while he stayed here rent-free was buying groceries and keeping food around that Justin could just grab and go.

"I had a banana before I went out and checked on the ewes."

It was nearly nine in the morning. She'd been up and working already, and technically so had he, but it was hard not to feel like she'd done more for Justin in her short time under the same roof than he had in the months he'd been staying.

"I earn my keep by cooking eggs," he said. "Do you want scrambled? Over easy? In a breakfast burrito?"

"Um…" Her gaze darted around the living room, touching on the mantel over the fireplace that held the pictures from her and Justin's childhood. When she focused on the short hallway to the kitchen, her forehead crinkled. "Sure, I'm starving, and a breakfast burrito sounds like it'll keep me for the rest of the day."

And it'd send him to a different room. "Major plans?"

The corners of her lips turned down, bordering on a frown. Others might not have caught it, but he had all of Brigit's expressions catalogued. "Job hunting."

He hadn't expected that answer, thought maybe she would be helping Justin with some task on the ranch or assisting her cousins with all the after-harvest work.

"Does Moore have a lot to offer?" Not for someone like Brigit. There were jobs, but no careers she'd be satisfied with. He couldn't picture her waiting tables, or even sitting behind a desk like her ex. She was always moving, elbow-deep in what needed to be done. Or according to Justin, studying, which must be coming to an end if she was talking about a job search.

A shadow crossed her face but was quickly replaced by her standard cool demeanor. "I won't be looking in Moore."

Her words were like a stealth bitch slap. After graduation, she had walked off the stage and out of his life. Since then, he'd been sustaining himself with glimpses of her and news of her well-being from her brother. She was home now, but that didn't mean she was his, and even if she were that didn't mean she would stay.

Two things she'd always been clear on: her intent to get out of Moore to make something of herself and her lack of interest in him since leaving.

"Right. I'll go get started." Hopefully she wouldn't notice how quickly he abandoned the topic of her job search.

In the kitchen, the tension drained out his body. It wasn't that he and Brigit couldn't get along or had a history of not being civil. No, the problem was that they'd blazed like a prairie fire, hot and fierce, and then she'd doused it with ice water in a second. He'd been left in the dark for the last ten years.

He retrieved the eggs from the fridge and started cooking, the work taking his mind off his woman problems, or rather lack thereof. Was she feeling as self-conscious as he was? She could be lost in her own drama, dealing with her own turmoil, and oblivious to his presence. They were nothing more than roommates. Barely even that.

He laid out three tortillas—one for each of them and a third for Justin, since the guy never cooked on his own. After getting the eggs ready, he fried some sausage and melted cheese in the wraps before rolling them and putting them on plates.

"Bridge, breakfast is ready." Did it really count as breakfast if it was almost ten in the morning? And why did calling her come so naturally?

She sauntered in, a navy-blue Walker Five hat squashed on her head with her ponytail hanging out the back. Soft denim molded over her legs and draped over her Ariat boots. Her purple sweatshirt was faded and one he recalled from their younger days. The few times he'd seen her since she'd left town, she'd been wearing slacks or dressier pants. It was nice seeing her in the clothing she'd grown up in. The look suited her, but he might be the only one who thought so.

"Wow, that smells delicious." She grabbed a couple paper towels to wrap the burritos in. "Thanks."

He twisted Justin's share in plastic wrap and set it in the fridge, then shot off a text to let his friend know there was food for him. He leaned against the counter to eat his own.

Brigit shifted her weight on her feet. "So, what do you have planned today?"

Was she nervous? She didn't take her food to the dining room and leave him alone. He shouldn't read anything into it. Just two old friends chatting. That's all this was.

"I'm gonna run home and check on my ladies." There was no house, but dammit, it was home, and he wasn't giving up on the cows. They hadn't given up on him, and he didn't have many people in his life who could say the same thing. "I need to figure out a time when it'll be good to work cattle so I can recruit some help."

Running a ranch by himself wasn't an issue, but there were certain times when it was an obstacle, like when he was moving them to another pasture, when it was time to work them, and then getting them loaded for sale… Yeah, being alone sucked. He went from a whole crew of coworkers that formed a cohesive unit at the firehouse to…himself.

"We know Justin will help," Brigit said. "Who usually pitches in?"

"Jesse, the guy who helped me out over the summer. Farah will probably be around too." Farah and her parents had always had his back. But Caleb would have had to dissolve the ranch if Jesse hadn't been stranded in town.

Brigit tipped her head. "That whole thing with Farah was kind of sudden."

"You mean her relationship with Jesse?"

"Yeah. I mean, she goes from seeing nobody, like ever, to seeing a guy with a record, to him going full hero during the tornado and them getting engaged."

Caleb smiled at her description. "He's a good guy, and he's really helped me out. I honestly don't know where I'd be right now without him." And since moving in with Farah, Jesse had ordered Caleb to quit paying him, claiming that it was the least he could do, since Caleb had given Jesse the space to put his life back on the right track in the first place. It had all worked to get Jesse and Farah together. Now, while Caleb was on duty, Jesse looked after his cattle and Farah helped when she was home.

"I always thought you would end up with her." Brigit took a bite like she wanted to keep from saying more.

Caleb's brows popped up and he stalled with his burrito halfway to his mouth. "Really? We've always been friends, nothing more."

"You don't see that too often." A faint pink stained the ridges of her cheeks. Did talking about him in a relationship with another woman embarrass her? She'd been the one engaged less than a week ago.

"Farah's one of my best friends." Like a sister from another mister. Though, with his mom's history, it wouldn't surprise him if he had half siblings running around, despite Mom swearing she'd taken care of that possibility. *I don't make the same mistake twice.* "There isn't that type of chemistry between us."

"I guess it's just not what you usually see." Brigit fiddled with a flap of tortilla.

"I'm surprised you thought that about us. You aren't around to notice who I spend my time with." *And I didn't think you cared.* He was going down a dangerous road, and he should stop. This was the first time he and Brigit had had an actual conversation in the last decade. But he couldn't get over her wondering about him and Farah, or that it was awkward for her to mention it.

Brigit set her plate down on the counter, her breakfast half eaten. "I know you and I had a thing when we were kids. I'm sorry it didn't turn out well, but our lives were going in different directions, and Mom helped me see that."

Had a thing? It had been more than a thing to him. She had been his past, present, and future. He would've given up everything, gone anywhere, to be with her. Sure, he'd had plans to stay in Moore and go to the fire academy. But for Brigit? He could've done that anywhere, in any town. There were fire departments literally everywhere, and even if he'd had a hard time finding one willing to look beyond the ear gauges and the punk hair and give a wild kid like him a chance, he would've found one. He would've made it happen. Because as long as he'd had Brigit, it all would've worked out.

"Our lives went in different directions because you walked away." He carefully set his plate down next to the sink and strode out of the kitchen before he could say something he'd regret. *Why couldn't you have talked to me? Wasn't that night special for you? Was I just an experience to get out of the way?*

This anger toward her was new. He'd dealt with the hurt, he lived with the pain of not knowing why he hadn't been good enough, and he'd gotten used to the loneliness of not settling for anything less than what he'd felt for her. To have her so casually mention what they had and how abruptly it had ended? Fury. Disappointment. Rejection. Two of those emotions were constant companions. The other was not.

He jogged up to his bedroom and gathered his straw cowboy hat and his work gloves. The only reason he still had these items were because they'd been in his truck during the storm. He'd been on duty while his house had blown through half the county.

Wiggling his fingers into his gloves, he thought over the conversation with Brigit. Her mom had pointed out that things wouldn't work between them? He'd always known Joan Walker didn't think highly of him. In high school, most of his friends' parents hadn't. Their opinions were a hazard of his parentage. To say his mom had issues would be an understatement. He'd lived mostly with his grandma and grandpa. He'd *wanted* to live with his grandparents despite the arguments with Mom about the situation.

His dad, or at least the guy he called Dad, had been along for the ride, but not ready for fatherhood. The man had been sucked into Mom's party orbit and either couldn't get out or didn't want to.

Caleb had never met his birth father. Apparently, the guy had left Moore long before Caleb was born—and long before his mom had figured out who his dad was. That, along with Mom's lifestyle and caustic personality, didn't endear her toward others. And people didn't understand—or didn't want to understand—that his mom was a product of her birth. She'd been adopted from an overcrowded orphanage in Colombia, where she'd gotten her basic human needs met, but not the TLC babies needed. According to Grandma, the orphanage had fed her but otherwise ignored her. Not that Mom shouldn't be held accountable for the swath of hard feelings she left in her path, but there'd never been any compassion there for her in the first place.

Reactive attachment disorder. Grandma had learned about it too late to seek out adequate therapy before Mom was off on a life of few attachments and little responsibility.

So the residents of Moore held it against Mom that she was wild, "loose," and less educated than the rest of them. And to someone like Joan Walker, those were all strikes against *him*.

He crushed the hat on his head. It acted like an instant signal to get to work. When he was on duty as a fireman, he looked the part and acted the part. He called this style his country-boy getup.

He fiddled with the collar of his light jacket, then dropped his hands and spun toward the door. Brigit didn't give a damn what he looked like. Her mother cared enough for both of them.

He wove through the house, got his boots on, grabbed a heavier jacket, and banged out the door. There was no sight or sound of Brigit. Hopping in his truck, he breathed a sigh of relief.

Why couldn't it have been simple between them? He'd thought it was back then.

A trip that normally loosened the knots of his neck and uncoiled the constant thread of tension he experienced on the job wasn't working today. He was too wound up, and seeing the gaping hole where his house once sat added to it.

The day of the storm had been a long shift. He'd had to be the hero for everyone else, then he'd come back to his place, back to nothing. All of his neighbors had been okay, everyone had survived, and even all his cattle had been accounted for, but the fact that his house had been obliterated was a constant stress in his life.

He made decent money with his job, but not build-a-brand-new-house money. And while the place had been old and a fifties throwback inside, he couldn't replace it. It'd been the only home he had known. Before Grandma had taken him in, he'd spent so many nights on strangers' couches, on the floor, or even a few times shoved into a closet for the night. Not that he'd admit that last one to anyone.

So, yeah. He'd been a little...unrefined...in school, for a while. Maybe some outbursts in high school. A fight or two —for perfectly valid reasons. No one insulted his mom, or anyone else he cared about.

Turning down the path to his place, he scanned his property. The outbuildings still sported damage from flying debris during the storm. Large hunks of paint were missing off the barn, and his shop's weathered siding was peppered with dents and puncture marks. There was nothing but a yawning hole where his house had been. Between the guys on the department and Justin's family and their connections, the rubble had been cleaned up quickly, and for a lot less than it would've otherwise cost.

Caleb opened the shop doors. He kept his beater pickup inside and he needed to move it. It was a good backup truck, but mostly he couldn't get rid of it because…memories. He was about to swing up into the tractor to stack hay bales when footsteps caught his attention.

"Hey, man." Jesse strode in, dressed in his typical black work boots and grease-stained jeans. He had a red ball cap on his head and a worn black North Face coat to ward off the chill. "Thought I saw you drive up."

Caleb's property was divided from Farah's by three rows of trees, most of which had survived the storm. "What were you doing out?"

"Electric fence went down, and the cows keep getting out. I believe Farah's dad now when he says yearling steers are the teenagers of the cattle world."

"Need a hand?"

"No, they're all back in and I'm going to set up a solar box today to power the fence."

"Nice." With his mechanical talents, Jesse was perfect for ranch life. Just having him as a neighbor had saved Caleb more money than he could fathom.

"Farah's dad was wondering when you want to work cattle."

"Let Derrick know I have next weekend off and we can coordinate. We do yours one day and then we do mine."

Jesse nodded and shoved his hands in his pockets. "Farah's off, too, so we were hoping that'd work. The more bodies the better. It's my first time with fall work so I don't know how much help I'll be."

"Justin won't mind lending a hand, and Brigit seems to like doing this stuff."

A dark brow cocked. "How's it going?"

He wasn't surprised Jesse knew about his troubles with Brigit. Jesse's wife was Caleb's sounding board. It wasn't like he could go to Justin and lament that Brigit wasn't talking to him after they'd slept together. And since he went out with coworkers and other law enforcement, Farah was often there to witness the tense interactions between him and Brigit.

"It's all right." It was torture. He planned to spend every daylight hour here so he didn't have to coexist with the woman of his dreams, who barely saw him as a friend. "Her breakup hasn't gotten uglier, so that's good." He shrugged and scrambled to change the subject before he started babbling about Brigit's daily activities and how it was good to see her in cowboy boots with her hair strung through a ball cap again. "I've been talking to builders."

Jesse tipped his head toward the spot where the house used to be. "Going with stick built?"

"I think it's the way to go, but it'll cost more." He couldn't build a less sturdy structure after what had happened.

"Keeping the same design?"

"I'll be lucky if I can afford the same square footage, but I'll try." The numbers weren't in his favor, though, not when the ranch was barely profitable. He rapped his knuckles on the tractor. "I'm going to stack bales. You guys have any I can throw around?"

"I did that yesterday. Derrick showed me how he likes them. I'm surprised you stack them so close to the yard."

"Because it's a fire hazard?" Caleb chuckled. "I have to balance my firefighter brain with my rancher side. Put them in small groups and if lightning hits, we won't lose the whole batch. It doesn't make sense to go out to the field every day for a bale and risk getting my tractor stuck in snow."

"I've driven past farms all my life and had no clue there was a reason to everything you guys do."

"You're one of us now. I don't think Farah will throw you out anytime soon."

"I make sure of it." Jesse toed the giant black tire of the tractor. "Come on over Saturday. We'll get started with the cattle when you're ready."

"See you then."

Jesse left, but Caleb didn't start his chores right away. One of his favorite things about meeting Jesse was that the man hadn't known him growing up.

A town like Moore was still small enough to remember all his antics. Maybe "antics" wasn't the right word. People still laughed about the time he and Justin rode horse through a drive-thru to get a couple of burgers. Or when he'd leapt barbed wire fences to outrun the cops busting their bonfire. People still brought up the way he and a few firemen buddies had decked out their coworker's car with streamers and a tin can tail a hundred feet long on his wedding night. Those were antics, and the town chuckled over them.

It was the strikes against him personally, like getting held back in first grade, that Moore never let anyone forget. They didn't pass kids who missed half the school year out "sick." When Social Services had pounded on the door, he'd gone to stay with Grandma, but the scholastic damage had been done.

Kids had long memories, and it was constantly pointed out that he should've been further along. Nor had kids been the only ones to say so. Joan Walker had brought up the fact at least once a year, often around Justin's birthday.

Oh that's right, you're a year older than Justin. I keep forgetting.

Caleb hadn't been allowed to forget. And Joan wasn't the only one who'd mentioned it over the years. Being held back shouldn't have been held against him. Kids got held back for all sorts of reasons.

He shook himself out of his own head and wandered out of the shop and across the round gravel drive. As he stared at the spot his future would be built on, he pictured the type of home he'd build. A giant house had never been his dream. No, his was a stable home—both in structure and livability. The builders he'd talked to had tried to convince him that one level was fine; then he could afford more amenities.

Was he being unreasonable to want a modern version of his grandparents' place? An homage to them, yes, but also a promise to himself that once he drove up and stepped inside, he wasn't going to be yanked back out.

BRIGIT'S FINGER hovered over the "learn more" button of the job opening. She sighed and closed the tab. After three days, she knew every position she was qualified for in the Minneapolis-St. Paul area. And she'd only applied for three of them.

Each time she passed over an opening, she'd come up with valid reasons. Too far from home. Too low of a wage for the hours demanded. Poor benefits. If Mom were here, she'd say not to expect to step through the door and earn the same as someone there for twenty years. Then in the next breath, she'd command Brigit not to settle for anything less than being a CEO.

She didn't need to start at the top, but upward mobility was a necessity. How long had she heard that she shouldn't settle for less and never ever block herself into a job going nowhere?

That advice had come from Dad. *Look at me, kiddo. I might be my own boss, but my raises are at the mercy of Mother Nature and she can be fickle. Find a place with a good reputation that allows you to grow.* Yet he'd raised two boys who'd gone out into the world and come right back because this was where they wanted to be.

The focus was on her. Did they realize it? Once Travis had come home and taken over as one of the Walker Five, Mom had upped her inquiries. *How's school going? Did you hit the dean's list again? Are you thinking about a graduate program?*

Then Justin had moved home from Denver. Their second prodigal son, a sheep rancher.

The questions had increased yet again. Half the reason Mom loved Oliver so much was that Brigit could concentrate on graduate school while Oliver...paid attention to other women, apparently.

Three jobs. That was enough. She wanted to run through weekend chores with Justin so they didn't double up. Offering to do his books had landed her a big "No. Got it taken care of." He probably didn't want her to learn the real reasons he was running back to Denver. He claimed he was wrapping up deals he'd started, unwilling to let his old company and clients down, and that might be true, but she wouldn't be surprised if one of the "deals" he wanted to close was a woman.

How did he manage such a level of privacy when Mom and Dad could pester her until she was listing every grocery run she'd been on and how it contributed toward her educational goals and study time?

Closing her laptop, she scooted off the bed and tiptoed to her bedroom door. Caleb had gotten home that morning and been gone all day. What was he spending his Friday doing?

The upper level was quiet. Giving herself a quick once-over, she adjusted her knit sweater before rolling her eyes. Caleb had seen her in pajamas and shit-covered jeans. He wasn't lusting after her when he was around.

She fiddled with the hem of her sweater. The lilac color was her favorite. Not long ago, she'd had her hair dyed the same shade. She'd loved it, but when it came time to interview for jobs, she'd made sure to go back to her natural color, followed by highlights. Look the part and all that.

This pair of jeans was clean. Justin hadn't had much work for her to do, which was good. It forced her to job hunt instead of wandering around outside finding tasks to perform, like checking the battery connections on the side-by-side that had decided to quit running.

Her stomach rumbled. She'd made a sandwich for lunch, but sitting in classes didn't inspire her appetite like tromping through the barns and pastures. And she didn't have Oliver subtly questioning how often and what she ate.

She puffed a strand of hair out of her face. How had she not smothered Oliver in his sleep? Was it guilt because he'd paid the bills while she'd gone to school? He hadn't helped with tuition or books, and she'd done all the housework and grocery shopping. She'd "taken care of him" in exchange for what? For paying the utility bills and for food—that she shopped for and cooked?

This time on her own was good for her. And the reason why she wasn't applying for work that didn't resonate with her.

Not that the three jobs she'd put in for inspired a hint of a thrill. At least she could cuddle barn cats while waiting to hear back.

She went downstairs and stalled at the bottom. Male voices drifted from the kitchen. Her pulse kicked up. Was Caleb home?

She listened. Yes, he and Justin were chatting. She glanced back up the stairs. No. Avoiding Caleb wasn't the answer to getting over him. If she could make it through being roommates with him, then she'd know she'd done the right thing all those years ago.

Because breaking things off with him had never felt right.

He was Moore to his bones. There was no way he would've left his grandparents for her. And no matter how aimless his mother was, she managed to stop back in Moore regularly to cause a ruckus and leave again. That was probably half the reason Caleb had never moved. Would his mom bother visiting him in another town? Had she bothered coming back to Moore once her own mother died?

Forcing herself to move, she walked into the kitchen. The smell of bacon grew stronger the closer she got.

Caleb was at the stove. Her bachelor brother had survived off takeout and delivery in Denver. Not an option in Moore. What'd he done before Caleb moved in?

"Mac and cheese," Caleb said. She had planted her gaze on the pot to avoid gaping at how good he looked.

He must've worn a hat all day. He'd brushed his dark, silky strands off his head, but they wanted to settle back into hat head. She liked way too much how his hair hugged his scalp and accentuated the cut of his jaw and the high cheekbones. He leaned against the counter as he stirred, his legs kicked out and his boots crossed.

"Homemade too," Justin added, the awe clear in his voice. Anyone who thought Caleb was taking advantage of Justin needed to witness this interaction. Justin kept peeking into the saucepan and shuffling his feet like a caged tiger at feeding time.

A mound of bacon sat next to the stove. She couldn't believe it had survived Justin's presence. "Mac and cheese with bacon?" It sounded good, delicious even, but she was born and raised in a ranching family. A meal was made around the meat, not the noodles.

"He mixed in grilled chicken. The bacon bits are on the side." Justin's smile reminded her of Christmas morning. He'd always had a hard time being patient.

"It's popular at work," Caleb said, taking the pan off the stove. "All done."

She helped Justin dig the plates and forks out. Caleb dished the food onto their plates, cheese strands stretching long. Her mouth watered, and her breath hitched when he got to her plate. Whenever she and Oliver had been at a buffet or potluck, he'd grabbed her the smallest slice of anything. Or his plate would have a generous serving while hers had a scant teaspoon.

Caleb spooned just as much, even more, on hers than the other two. Then he piled more bacon on top. The corner of his mouth tipped up and her belly flipped. That was Caleb. The smallest gestures had always made her feel the most accepted.

"I'd say the recipe is secret, but I just throw shit together," he said.

They carried their food to the dining room. It was the first time the three of them had sat down together for a meal. They were usually like three balls in motion, bouncing around each other and rolling through the house for meals and sleep.

"This needs a beer," Justin announced, turning back to the kitchen. "Bridge?"

Her gaze automatically strayed to Caleb, like she'd done with Oliver. Searching for approval and deciding whether she wanted to defend her choice of drink and the calories she consumed.

Caleb caught her gaze, a beat of surprise going through his eyes, like he'd expected her to ignore him. "Beer makes it even better."

She couldn't fight her grin. "Melted cheese and bacon needs to be better?"

"You'll see." Justin disappeared and she dug in, blowing on the first bite before stuffing it in her mouth. That sandwich had been hours ago and she'd ridden horse part of the morning.

Her eyelids drifted closed and a moan escaped. She chewed and enjoyed the mingling of the best flavors in the world. The chicken he'd used was actually grilled, not dumped from a package and warmed, or even cooked with the broiler. When had he grilled?

Opening her eyes, she met Caleb's gaze. His fork was poised over his plate, a heap settled on it, but he watched her. She flicked her tongue across her lip to catch any stray strands of cheddar. His gaze dipped to her mouth. The air sizzled between them. Was he still attracted to her? As much as she was to him and hadn't been able to admit until now?

Justin rounded the entrance, three longnecks in his hands. "I hope you made enough for leftovers for a week."

Caleb jerked his attention back to his plate. "Maybe not a week, but it might get us through the weekend."

Justin passed out the beer and settled in. "It'll be perfect for after working cattle."

About to take a drink, Brigit put the bottle back down. She'd always looked forward to working cattle. As she'd gotten older, she'd been promoted from running the calves up the shoot to recording the data behind tag numbers and shots. The last few times Cash had worked cattle, she'd come home and helped administer the vaccines. "Do you need help?"

Justin held his hands up. "It's not my call. I'm helping the Jameses and then Caleb."

Would Farah want her around? Brigit suspected Farah was the only one besides her, Caleb, and Mom who knew even part of what had happened when they were younger.

But a weekend of hard labor and working cattle sounded divine. She'd rather have her head hit the pillow after a full day and aching muscles than be restless in bed and worried about how little she wanted to apply anywhere.

"Think she'd mind?" she asked Caleb. She didn't need to be BFFs with Farah in order to lend a hand.

Caleb's jaw flexed, a fine crinkle marring his forehead. "I guess I could ask. If you were there on Saturday, it'd free her up to teach Jesse the process. But, yeah, you can come out to my place Sunday and throw in with the rest of us. I have about sixty calves to tag and vaccinate."

A triumphant smile curved her lips. She went from dreading another day of scouring online classifieds to pure excitement. "Put in a good word with Farah for me? I can't sit around on the computer for another day."

"Find anything good?" Justin asked.

"A few positions that looked promising." She avoided looking at Caleb. Talking about leaving Moore when she'd just moved back rubbed a wound that she hadn't known was so raw. The year she graduated, she'd hung around all summer, helping Dad. Mom had done all the dorm setup and practically packed for her.

"Where at?" Caleb's voice was low, his gaze direct.

"Two in Minneapolis and one in St. Paul." She said it in the same tone that she used when she discussed her future with others. Confidence mixed with optimism. The effect came naturally now, even if she lacked the youthful exuberance she used to have.

Justin pushed his empty plate away and reclined in his chair. His dirty blond hair was ruffled, and his black T-shirt was faded and a few washes away from disintegrating. She'd met up with him once in Denver. This Justin was the complete opposite of Denver Justin, and she was probably the only one to have witnessed it.

"Have you thought about Alexandria or Fergus Falls?" he asked. "Even Fargo isn't that far away."

"They're still a little too small to have the variety in job opportunities I'm looking for." Out of the corner of her eye, she saw Caleb look away. Did he think she was being uppity for discriminating against small populations when she'd been born and raised in a town of less than ten thousand?

Justin nodded and scrubbed his face. "I get it. Might as well set up in the place you want to live in."

She opened her mouth, then clamped it shut. She'd been so close to saying she didn't want to live in Minneapolis, but that was where the work was. It'd just muddy the waters.

"Good luck with the job hunting." Caleb nodded to her and to Justin before he stood. He carried his plate and lifted Justin's to stack with his.

Brigit straightened. They'd barely finished eating and he was leaving already? The urge to beg him to stay was strong, but she pressed her lips together.

"I'm washing, remember?" Justin called. His beer was half full. He wouldn't be going anywhere until it was gone.

"I'll wash." Brigit rose with her plate in one hand and her beer in the other. She tried not to rush after Caleb, but she couldn't help wanting to see him one more time before he left.

His back was to her and despite Justin's warning, he was rinsing the dishes. The dishwasher door hung open.

"You spoil him." She waited next to him.

He chuckled. "It's the least I can do."

"You're going to have to leave some work for me to do." She nudged his arm with her elbow, ignoring the flare of warmth blooming across her skin. "Or you're going to make me look bad."

He glanced at her and grinned. "You're related. The baby sister gets away with everything."

"I'm the baby by two minutes."

"I thought it was two and a half?"

"The way Justin acts sometimes, those thirty seconds are like five years."

They fell silent. The short banter between them could sustain her for weeks, but he was right here and she didn't want it to end.

"Are you sure it's okay if I help out this weekend?"

He shut off the water and met her gaze. The air stilled between them. His eyes mesmerized her. They were the softest brown, like a baby calf's coat when it was still fluffy with a little curl. "It'll be all right. I'll shoot Farah a text. You know she'll tell me if it's an issue."

"You told her about us, didn't you?" she murmured.

Caleb's gaze shot over her shoulder, but Justin was probably nursing his beer and scrolling through his phone at the table. "It's not like I could talk to your brother."

"I appreciate it. My family is in enough of my business."

Caleb turned from her to stack the plates in the dishwasher. "They love you."

To anyone else, his explanation would sound like he was reassuring her, but she knew him and his past. The wistfulness in his words wasn't lost on her.

"How's your mom?"

He spoke as he arranged silverware and glasses from breakfast. She backed up a step, using the excuse of giving him room when she was only putting enough space between them to admire the firmness of his ass as he bent over.

"I guess they're in Texas. Mom's cleaning houses and Dad's doing landscaping."

"Good. Sounds like they're doing well."

"It always does." He straightened, and she yanked her gaze to his face. While he was shoving his hair off his forehead, she ogled the flex of his bicep. "She makes sure of it. I don't think they burn out of the party crowd as fast down there."

How could he be so accepting of a woman who clearly

put her own interests before him? But then he was here, chatting with her. But the difference was that she refused to lead him on like Adele Cruise did. She wasn't going to come and go from Caleb's life.

So why was she lingering in the kitchen? "Well, I'd better get back to it."

His half smile died. Kicking the dishwasher door up, he clicked it closed. "Yeah, I'm going to head to bed. I have to study."

"What?" She hadn't meant to sound so surprised.

A flash of hurt crossed his face, but it was gone in a second. "I'm a few credits away from finishing my bachelor's."

"Degree?"

His jaw tensed. He didn't irritate easily, but the chiseled cut of his jaw made it easy to tell. She hadn't meant to sound so surprised. "I've been taking online courses. It's a small town, but there are opportunities for promotion."

Caleb had always known what he wanted to do. Growing up, he'd told any teacher or classmate or anyone with ears willing to listen what he wanted to be: a fireman and a rancher. Now he was doing both. So what was he going to school for? "That's cool. In what?"

"Emergency management."

She cocked her head. "Not fire science or…fire something? You were always the kid who wanted to be a firefighter."

A faint smile ghosted his lips. Every Halloween, he'd worn a red jacket and fire hat. Every career day—fireman. And on their field trips to the fire department, he'd been first in line, raising his hand until they cut the questions off.

"My associate's is in fire science, but I thought a related degree that would allow more job diversity was smart."

"Very smart," she echoed. She hadn't even known he'd

gotten a two-year degree. He'd been so single-minded in his career track she hadn't thought outside of it, either. But he was focused and working for more.

"So..." He pointed over his shoulder. "I'm gonna hit the books. You can take credit for the dishes if you want." He sent her a little wink that ignited a spark in her belly.

To distract herself, she put detergent in the dishwasher and started it. It was a crappy effort.

CHAPTER 5

Today would normally be a fun day. Even through the dirt and the manure and the hard work, and the aching toe that had gotten ground down by a hoof, Caleb liked working cattle.

Brigit made it hell.

Her voice echoing behind him. Her laughs as she joked around with Farah's dad. And how did she smell that good when they'd been in the barn half the day running calves? Justin had left an hour ago. His friend's absence only made Caleb more aware of her.

He adjusted his hat and concentrated on his task. Jesse was manning the hydraulic gate he'd already had to repair twice today. Caleb was recording and giving vaccinations.

He let the last calf go and took his hat off to wipe the dust off his brow. Farah herded the steer to the proper pasture. It'd get loaded in the next few weeks and hauled to the sales barn. He glanced out the open barn doors. The sun was sinking in the horizon, but they'd finished before dark. That was always welcome.

"You earned your money today." Caleb grinned at Jesse.

They'd worked past dark yesterday. Farah's operation was a little larger, since it was her and her dad running it. With Jesse, they planned to grow it even more.

Caleb experienced a pinch of envy. He'd like to expand his ranch, maybe even pair with a genetics company to raise breeders, but when it was just him, he couldn't advance in his profession and take on more duties on his ranch. Right now if it failed, it was just him that suffered.

"This shit is unreal." Jesse stared at Farah as she entered the barn and crossed to where her dad and Brigit were unhooking gates. "I expected more chaos, but it wasn't bad."

"Some years, things get exciting, but Grandpa taught me quick to weed out the problem cows. The older cows have enough experience they don't get worked up. Then the calves don't get too worried. I've had some of these for seven years."

"What are you going to do with the four in the pen?"

One cow had broken her leg, two hadn't calved in two years, and one had hoof rot from steeping herself in the spring-fed pond too long. There was always one in the bunch who liked to marinate in the pond until she got sick.

"The hoof rot we can treat. The others…"

Jesse flashed a grin. "From feed to fork?"

"That's why we don't name them." Respect the animal, care for it, but don't get attached. He needed to make as much as he could off each head to keep the ranch running. Grandpa had been savvy about squeezing every penny out of the stock he had, but he hadn't been as good at growing the ranch. Caleb tried to keep improving, but he always seemed behind the curve.

"Give me a call when you round 'em up to sell." Jesse sauntered away.

"Thanks, man."

Derrick called across the barn. "I'm gonna get grilling.

You kids go get cleaned up and come over in forty-five. I know we worked up an appetite."

Jesse and Farah went with him, leaving Caleb alone with Brigit. Her cheeks were rosy, and her breath puffed out. Once the cows had cleared out, the temperature in the barn had plummeted.

She'd ridden here with Justin and since he was gone, Caleb didn't look forward to sharing the small cab of his pickup with her. Justin's *house* was too small when they were both in it together.

"I can give you a ride to the house to clean up," he offered. "You're coming back to eat, right?"

She took off her work gloves. "I don't know. I hate to keep feeling like I'm intruding."

She'd gotten along with Farah and Jesse. Not super friendly, but a step above business relations. Farah's dad liked to take everyone under his wing and hadn't missed the chance to shoot rapid-fire questions at Brigit about their farm and ranch operation. Even Caleb had been stunned by her knowledge of the operation's history, its growth, and her family's plans for expansion. She didn't run it, but she'd paid attention her entire life. She didn't just do the work and collect an easy paycheck from her kin.

"It's a tradition to get together after the cattle are done." It was like a goodbye to summer. The cows were in their winter pastures closer to home, any fields were hopefully in —though Caleb didn't have time to grow his own silage to supplement the cattle—and a payday from cattle sales was hopefully soon to come. "You helped all weekend. Come eat. Unless you have plans."

Come to think of it, the two weeks she'd been at Justin's, she hadn't gone out once. Not with friends, not with her family, not at all. She worked and applied for work.

She grimaced. "My friends have never been to Moore. And I think Oliver got them in the breakup."

"Ah, it's like that." He wanted to ask about her friends *from* Moore. Didn't she have people she'd kept in contact with over the years? He lived here, but there were still guys who came back to visit that would hit him up to go out.

Thinking back to when they were kids, he couldn't come up with a group of girls she'd hung out with. She was friendly with everyone, sometimes painfully so. But many times, she'd formed a trio with him and Justin.

As if answering the questions he didn't ask, she said, "Pathetic, I know. But I was always nose-deep in a textbook. Socializing wasn't on my mind."

Yet she'd managed to have a couple of long-term boyfriends and even get engaged. He couldn't be surprised. A tall stunner like her would attract men like flies. A good analogy, since from what he'd heard about Oliver, the men she'd dated had treated her like shit. There wasn't one Justin had approved of.

On top of that, she thought she was pathetic for no longer being around people who made relationships one-sided.

"Being focused isn't pathetic. And I'm guessing that if the friends prefer Oliver, then you're better off without them."

Her smile was slow, and she shook her head. "I never thought about it like that, but…"

He waited for her to finish, but she didn't. The gravity in her expression prompted him to ask, "But what?"

She shrugged. "They're nice people, but there was always this subtle undercurrent of competition. Like when we moved back here, Oliver made me promise not to say anything until he'd landed a job. When he told people why we'd moved back, he made it sound like he was doing his family friend a solid by working for him in Normandy.

'Closer to the parents and all that. They're not getting any younger.'"

The sarcastic note in her voice reminded him of the old Brigit. The one who pretended to be the good girl around her mother but cussed at the cattle when they acted stupid and bluntly stated what was on her mind. Had her cousins ever seen that side of her, or was it just him and Justin? Hell, had Travis?

"I'm sure he thought he was the expert in a lot of things," he said.

"Well, he can try to impress what's her name."

The divorced insurance adjuster he'd been having the affair with. "Better her wasting her time with him than you."

"Logically I know that, but it still hurts."

He crossed to her. The dim lights in the barn cast shadows across her face that matched her expression. "I know it does. You trusted someone, and he let you down."

She didn't move away. "I moved back to Moore for him." She screwed her face up. "Mom didn't even pester me about it because it seemed like he helped me a lot with school." She lowered her voice to mimic Oliver. "'We have to save money. Your school costs too much and Dad can use his connections to get me a job. You do your part and get a job in the Twin Cities and I'll worry about the rest.'" She snorted and looked away, but her eyes shimmered with extra moisture.

"It was his idea to move back but he blamed you?" He didn't bother mentioning the fact that coming home didn't equate with failure.

"I kept going to school, so…"

"Bridge." She lifted her gaze to his. The rim of gold in her blue irises glittered with a sheen of tears. "It's not who did or didn't do what, it's how he made you feel. It was wrong."

She cocked her head. Her forehead wrinkled like she was fighting to keep the tears from spilling. A sniffle echoed through the barn, but a small smile graced her full lips. "When'd you get so wise?"

She was trying to lighten the mood, but her question only grated on him. His job wasn't just fighting fires. He was there when bad shit happened to people, regardless of whether they were good or bad. "Hazards of the job, I guess."

Compassion filled her eyes. "Oh, Caleb. I never think about what you must go through."

She drifted closer and feathered her fingers down his cheek. He hadn't meant to get so deep into the tragedies of his job. This discussion wasn't about him, but he'd gone from dealing with his own childhood to bearing witness to life going to hell for others, and except for some counseling through work when a particularly bad incident happened, he had no one to talk to.

"I didn't, uh…" he said gruffly. "I didn't mean to get all serious."

"But what you do is serious. It's a lot more serious than a cheating ex." She hadn't removed her hand, settling her warm palm on his shoulder instead. The brims of their hats nearly touched.

"I deal with those too." He grinned. This time he was the one trying to lighten the mood. Because if Brigit didn't back away, he was going to tilt his head a few inches to the right and try to kiss her. No matter whether she let him or shunned him, it would ruin him. "Their fights are Farah's territory, but one time, a couple crashed while fighting about his affairs and they were still arguing when my crew showed up."

Brigit giggled. "Sorry. I know it's not funny."

"They were both okay, but her door wouldn't open and his was pinned against a telephone pole. And they were still screaming at each other."

"I'm glad that time turned out well. At least for you."

He nodded, a lump forming in his throat. She was so close, her body heat reaching for his. It would be so easy to wrap his arms around her waist. They were both dirty, standing in a barn littered with cow shit, but all he wanted to do was hold her and never let her go.

"Bridge." He had to get out of this situation and break this spell she had over him. Her rejection had destroyed him once. He wasn't in a place to weather it again. "You coming with me to Farah's?" There. That was a good place to start.

She drew in a breath and dropped her hand from his shoulder. He instantly missed the contact.

"I *am* hungry." There was still a note of uncertainty.

"I mean, if you can tolerate not having Walker beef."

She grinned and lightly punched him on the shoulder. "Now I'm going to have to go and scope out the competition."

"You'd better come with. I don't think Derrick will forgive me if I don't bring the one person who can talk cattle as much as him."

She laughed, and they wandered to his pickup. He should've made life easy on himself and dissuaded her from coming with him. But he would find a way to endure being inches from her without trying to kiss her and making an ass of himself. All he had to do was make it through the night.

It was getting late, and the temperature was dropping below freezing, but Farah had opened the shop doors and fired up the electric heater. Brigit's coat was in Caleb's truck, but she was comfortable in the sweater she'd thrown on.

If her college friends could see her now. She was in an old university sweater and a clean pair of jeans she usually wore around the farm, with a pair of boots that weren't muddy.

Her clothing was snugger than the last time she'd come home to help work cattle or bring the harvest in, but all that meant was that she was the same size she'd been when she'd left home.

The food! Body-conscious Oliver and his protein shakes and mixed green salads. All were fine, but Lord, she'd missed her beef, and not the lean cuts. Mr. James had grilled a "rib eye and a spare" for each of them. She'd eaten both. Because life was too short to limit her intake to eight ounces.

She might regret that motto in the morning.

But for tonight she was full of quality cuts, she had a cold beer in her hand, and she'd been cornered by Mr. James and his wife. Caleb was laughing at the folding table with Farah and Jesse. Justin had claimed he had a late conference call and couldn't make it.

Brigit caught herself looking at Caleb again and how the sweatshirt he wore draped over his broad shoulders and tapered down to his waist. She tore her gaze off him and focused on her own conversation.

"Black Angus don't get as big as we need." Mrs. James was talking, proving she could still command a room. Before her stroke, she'd been the sheriff, but her gaze was direct and while her words came slower now, she made them count—when she could get a word in edgewise. Brigit and Mr. James hadn't let up discussing sales-barn politics and Big Agriculture conspiracy theories.

Mr. James nodded. "I don't think purebred is the way to go. The best cattle I've ever raised were Black Angus crossed with Charolais."

"For a small operation like this, I think mixed genetics is the best," Brigit agreed. "But I think it'd be interesting to see what a ranch like Caleb's could do if they partnered with a genetics company and raised stock cattle."

"It's tempting to switch to stock cattle." Mr. James huffed.

"Especially the way beef sales have slowed down. But we're too small to catch their notice. The Walker Five could get into negotiations though."

"I've put a bug in Caleb's ear about it." Brigit grinned. "Everyone thinks he's laid-back, but when it comes to the ranch portion, he's interested in expanding."

"Good for him."

"But between trying to build a house and balancing the ranch and his job, he's a little stuck on what he's able to do." He wanted to do more with this place, and she had so many ideas. But it wasn't her place.

Story of her life.

Mr. James nodded. Caleb's financial dilemma was the story of a lot of ranchers' lives. "I wish I could get to more ag shows in the winter, but it's getting harder to travel. But you know how it goes. Moore's too small to attract much of any workshops or conferences."

Mr. James glanced at his wife and did a double take. The more the night went on, the less animated her features were. "It's past our bedtime. What d'ya say, honey?" He didn't wait for an answer but hopped up to help her stand. Arm in arm, they walked out of the shop. "You kids stay as long as you want. And don't worry about the noise. Our neighbors moo all night."

Brigit wandered over to the folding table, trying not to stare at the tender way Mr. James treated his wife. Her chest constricted. The Jameses were in it for the long haul, their lives and their careers in Moore.

Why hadn't Brigit wanted that?

Right. CEO ambitions and all that—after the whole law school debacle.

Caleb pulled out the chair next to him. "Say the word and we'll go. Farah and I are used to being up at all hours and we tend to keep Jesse past his bedtime."

"I'm fine." Brigit took her seat. This night was better than any bar she'd ever gone to.

Jesse had his arm slung across the back of Farah's chair and she snuggled into him. Seeing how she acted around her fiancé made Brigit wonder how she'd ever thought Farah and Caleb had a thing for each other. They were close, but there was nothing physical between them.

Farah broke the silence. "Too bad Justin couldn't make it, but he was always the mysterious one."

"That's a good word for it." Brigit set her drink down. The others were looking at her, and just like that, any small talk skills she possessed vanished. These three were clearly good friends. She was the odd one out. Like always. Only Caleb didn't overwhelm a conversation like Oliver had.

Caleb chuckled. "I don't know what international marketing entails, but I think he's really a secret agent still working out of Denver."

"A secret agent sheep farmer?" Brigit asked.

"The best cover."

"Remember when you two used to spy on me?" Farah asked.

Jesse leaned forward. "Wait. I have to hear this."

Caleb held up a finger. "One, we were, like, ten."

"Thirteen," Farah said.

"And two"—Caleb stuck up a second finger—"it just seemed like a good idea at the time. We asked you to ride horse and you said you were busy. Clearly, you don't know the curiosity that inspires in a teenage kid."

"I wanted to ride horse without you two dicking around and getting me in trouble."

Caleb held up another finger. "Three, we didn't know how *not* to get into trouble." His serious expression dissolved into a grin. He took off his cowboy hat and brushed his hand over his hair. "Oh, man. I can't believe your mom didn't ban me from your property."

Farah shook her head. "Mom and Dad never would've done that. Mom always said she'd been around enough bad people to know you're not one of them."

Brigit fought to keep her smile from dying. *Mom and Dad would've never done that.* How simply Farah said it, and with all the confidence in the world.

That boy is going to bring you down with him. What if he got you pregnant? How hard would college be then, and would he even stick around? He might be staying in Moore, but it doesn't mean he'll stay with you. Look at Adele Cruise. Do you want that for yourself, Brigit?

Mom had known Caleb for as long as Mrs. James.

"I wouldn't have blamed her though." Caleb's own grin was still in place. "I was a shit."

"Sometimes," Farah agreed. "A lovable shit."

Brigit eyed Caleb out of the corner of her eye. He'd made the claim so simply. He wouldn't have blamed Mrs. James if she'd written him off as a lost cause and forbidden her daughter to have anything to do with him, like that was his lot in life and he accepted it.

"Why a fireman?" Jesse asked.

Farah cocked her head, like she'd never thought to ask. Neither had Brigit. "Caleb" and "fireman" had just gone together since she'd known him.

His expression turned grim and a flash of pain went through his eyes. "You haven't met my mom, Jesse, but being responsible was never her strong suit. Neither was parenting. I was four when we were staying at her boyfriend's place in Fergus Falls and they both fell asleep—well, passed out—with a cigarette burning away. And I wouldn't be surprised if they'd each had more than a smoke lit."

Brigit's eyes went wide. "Oh my God. Did you all get out

okay?" Obviously he had, and his mom had, but what about the boyfriend?

"They did." His jaw was tight, his eyes pinched. "I woke to smoke and shouting, and I did what most terrified kids do and crawled under the bed." The shop was the quietest it'd been all night as the three of them were riveted by Caleb's story. "I should've been terrified. The fireman looked like an alien, but I always was a weird kid and when he held his hand out, I went." Caleb shrugged. "When he carried me out, I felt like no flames in the world could touch us."

Brigit stared at him. One simple question. How had she not thought to ask why he'd wanted to be a firefighter?

"Damn, dude." Jesse shook his head.

"Yeah," Caleb agreed. "That was the first time I was taken away from Mom."

All three of them blinked. Taken away? As in by Social Services? Had Brigit been the most selfish friend in the universe to not know this about Caleb? Had he ever told Justin?

"What?" Farah asked, her expression matching the incredulity all of them felt.

Farah's ignorance made Brigit feel a smidge better.

"Mom was too wasted to remember I was in the house. It was a neighbor who reported having seen a kid running around that day. I was only taken away twice before I went to live with my grandparents. I guess it's not something I ever talked about."

"*Only* twice?" Brigit said. He sounded so nonchalant about it.

"Mom moved back so I could start school, since her address was still here. Then after I was held back in first grade, Grandma gave her an ultimatum. I live with them, or Mom would get reported."

Farah narrowed her eyes. "Reported for what?"

Caleb chuckled. He was the only one who saw humor in any of this. "Who knows? The cops, Social Services, the IRS? Could've been any of them."

"Grandpa and Grandma Cruise were good people," Farah said.

"The best," Caleb agreed. "Not many people have to deal with what they went through, and at the time no one understood Mom's attachment disorder well, much less how to raise a kid with it. So Mom never got the help she needed, despite my grandparents' efforts."

Brigit was still staring at Caleb. He talked so plainly about his past, a man comfortable with himself. She wanted to throw her arms around him, comfort him, but he didn't need it. He didn't need her.

The realization sank in. Caleb had never needed her. She'd left him, and he'd followed his dreams to the letter. He was in the career he wanted and had carried on his grandparents' ranch.

Wasn't that the ultimate point Mom had made, even if she hadn't known it at the time? Caleb was strong enough to be on his own, but Brigit wasn't.

She switched her gaze to Farah. The other woman was laughing as she and Caleb reminisced about his grandparents. The woman had also stayed in Moore and made a name for herself. She, too, lived with her parents—sort of. Her home apartment was a mother-in-law suite built into the shop. But she had a full-time job as a deputy and helped her dad ranch.

Mom had told her about the hubbub over Farah's fiancé. Her voice had dripped with disdain, and all his heroic deeds —like saving Farah and Caleb's neighbor post-tornado— would never redeem him in her eyes for what he'd done to Brigit's cousin's place. It didn't matter that her cousin had forgiven Jesse or that Jesse was slowly paying him back.

When you're a lawyer, you can make sure guys like that stay in prison.

I'm not going to be that kind of lawyer, Mom.

Brigit wasn't going to be any kind of lawyer. Looking around the table, she was the only one who hadn't amounted to anything.

"Are you sure you're okay?" Caleb turned off the highway, sneaking a glimpse at Brigit's wan face in the glow of the dashboard lights.

"Yeah. Just tired I guess."

One thing about Bridge was that she was a shitty liar. He'd suggested they head back to Justin's when she'd grown noticeably quiet after the talk about his childhood.

She was probably marveling over what a close call she'd had. Not only did he not have a roof over his head, he had no reliable family left alive.

Or did she feel sorry for him? Pity was the *numero uno* reason he never talked about his life. He got enough of that, and even though his mom had made terrible mistakes and horrible decisions, he hated how her failures were all anyone saw.

There wasn't much else to see, to be honest, but it was the kid in him. The one who'd sat by Grandma and sifted through Mom's old school artwork and heard the stories of Mom's first Christmas, the school play when she was ten, and how she'd loved riding horse with Grandpa.

But enough of Mom. He'd dwelled on his past too much lately. Perhaps it was Brigit back in his life, or rebuilding the house he'd grown up in.

He sailed down the gravel road, his brights lighting up the ditches with the heat kicking out the chill of a Minnesota November.

He'd just opened his mouth to comment on how she'd impressed Derrick when a flicker of movement in the grass caught his eye. Letting off the gas, he poised his foot over the brake. A deer with a modest-sized rack darted onto the road, saw his pickup, and stopped, right smack in front of him.

Caleb stomped on the brake, but he didn't have time to lay on the horn. His seat belt tightened around him, and Brigit's head flew forward, her hair swirling around her face as her belt caught her. A thud sounded over the skittering of gravel, and the body of the buck bounced onto his hood and slid off the driver's side.

A whirl of dust surrounded them and quickly cleared away.

"Shit." At least they were okay. It'd been a buck, but from his quick glimpse, the deer had been young. Big enough to dent and scratch his hood, though.

"Thank goodness it didn't come through the windshield." Brigit unhooked her seat belt and leaned over to peer out his window, but the animal had landed out of the glow of his headlights.

Caleb guided the vehicle to the side of the road, parked, and turned on his hazards. "I just hope it died on contact." He didn't like the idea of killing the animal, but it was better than letting it suffer.

He dug out his phone and hopped out. Brigit exited behind him. The road was empty and the Walkers who lived on each side were probably snug in their beds. Dillon's and

Cash's houses were still a half mile away. The lights shouldn't bother them.

Brigit rounded on the deer, the light on her phone shining on the face. The creature was on its side, its head at an angle few mammals could tolerate. She shone her light over the eyes.

"Dead."

"At least there's that." He called the dispatcher. "Hey, Evie. I hit a deer by Dillon Walker's. Can you send someone? Perfect."

His insurance might not require a report, but after his house, he didn't want to take chances. His rates were already going to skyrocket.

Fuck.

He grabbed a bigger flashlight from his vehicle. The damage was isolated to the front. He cast the beam over the hood.

Double fuck. The antlers had gouged and scratched the paint, his grill was busted, and there was a dent the size of the buck in the hood. It'd look worse in the morning.

But he'd seen worse accidents with smaller deer.

"Oh my. Look at that." Brigit crossed to him. "I'm so sorry."

Yep. "At least I slowed a little, or he might've taken one of us with him."

"I never saw him."

"I did, but not in time." He sighed. Brigit rubbed his back. Deer accidents were common enough that everyone in Moore knew what came next: spending money to fix his vehicle. A lot of it. But they were okay. That was what mattered.

Headlights lit up the distance. He turned, almost wanting more time alone with her. It was cold and dark, but he barely noticed either.

"That was fast," Brigit murmured.

"Must've been in the area."

The patrol car parked behind his pickup, but at a slight angle to shine its headlights on the carcass. Caleb wished Farah were on duty, but he got along with the other deputies too.

Brigit sidestepped out of the glare of the headlights and hovered on the side of the road by his pickup.

Cote Yellowbird unfolded his tall frame and tipped his hat. "Cruise, you hitting my deer?"

Caleb grinned despite the pit in his stomach at his draining finances. "This here is a city deer, Deputy."

Cote chuckled. "You're my fourth deer-on-car action this week. 'Tis the season." He wandered through the scene, shining his flashlight on Caleb's bumper, then on the deer. The beam of light lifted to where Brigit waited by the pickup. She gave a little wave.

"Cote, do you know Brigit Walker?"

"The name only. Nice to meet you, ma'am."

"Wish it were under better circumstances." She smiled but didn't cross to join them.

Caleb gauged her stance. Was she just cold, or trying not to be seen with him?

Cote interrupted his speculation. "Tell you what. I'll write you a permit if you wanna keep it."

Loading Justin's freezer with fresh roadkill venison would assuage his guilt slightly, but the logistics were hard to figure out. Grandpa had never been a hunter, and Caleb didn't use his guns for anything other than the occasional rabid skunk or coyote stalking his calves. "I don't have a field kit."

"I always carry one, just in case, you know, a motorist turns down the offer." Cote's long strides ate the distance to his trunk. "You can borrow it. Lemme know when you're on duty and I'll swing by and grab it."

"Aren't you afraid I'll spill the secrets behind the cuts of moose you donate to the firemen's wild game feed?"

Cote flashed a smile as he handed over a leather bag full of tools. "I didn't hear any of you complaining."

"As long as it was fresh when you found it."

Cote snorted. "It was probably in better shape than the vehicle that hit it. I'm sure it was a bunch of kids out drinking, and I'd love to hear how they explained to their parents why there was a dent the size of a seven-hundred-pound moose in their hood. They were only able to drive away because it'd been a young bull." He murmured into the radio clipped to his collar. "Well, I'll leave you to it."

Their surroundings dimmed as Cote swung his patrol car back to do a K-turn and leave.

Brigit had been quiet the whole time, like she'd been trying to fade into the background. Easy to do in the middle of the night.

His jaw tensed. Cote was perceptive, but he wasn't a guy who'd jabber about who he'd seen with whom. Caleb could reassure Brigit, but fuck it.

He'd been her dirty little secret before. At least now he knew how the game was played.

THE SIXTY-WATT BULB in the wooden toolshed was adequate enough for stringing up the carcass until there was time to process it. Old and musty, the shed was the best place to keep the meat protected from predators, or from scaring the sheep. When it was ready, it'd be processed into venison and sausage. Quality meat from an unfortunate accident.

Brigit shut the door behind them and stepped in to help Caleb string up the carcass.

This wasn't the worst night she'd ever spent with a guy. That award went to…what was his name? Jonathon. The night she'd ordered the half-pound mushroom and swiss burger with fries because she was so sick of grilled chicken and side salads.

After dinner, they'd gone to a play, and then since it was their third date, they'd gone back to his place. He'd been getting handsy while she'd been thinking something was terribly wrong.

As she puked into his toilet, her thoughts vacillated between mortification and gratitude that she'd made it to the bathroom instead of spewing over the furniture. But Jonathon commented on how the amount of food she'd eaten must've upset her stomach. Then he called her a cab. That she'd had to pay for.

So cleaning a deer with Caleb until the wee hours of the morning? Not so bad.

Actually, it was the most fun she'd had on a weekend in a long time, and it ended in a freezer full of food. He'd been quiet since the deputy had left.

Caleb lifted his chin toward his pickup parked outside of the open shed door. "I can clean up the pickup bed and the tools, if you want to shower first."

"I'll help with the cleanup. Justin's not around so I can use his bathroom." Her brother kept mysterious hours, but he was still a single guy. When he didn't come home at night, she had one guess as to where he was. She didn't know who, and in this small town, she preferred not to.

Caleb nodded and moved the pickup. He'd gotten quieter as the night wore on. No doubt the financial ramifications were setting in, and on top of him losing his house. That was enough to make anybody quiet.

Together, they sprayed off his pickup. Her fingers were radiating cold by the time they were done but she didn't rush inside. No matter how odd her night had been, she didn't want it to end.

Caleb tossed the bag full of now clean tools inside and slammed the pickup door. "I don't think my doors will freeze shut."

She closed the shop door. "You don't work in the morning, do you?" He hadn't mentioned anything, but why would he to her?

"I work Tuesday and Friday this week. So I get to deal with insurance and repair estimates tomorrow. At least I have my old beat-up truck working so I can still get around."

"Oh." Such an empty word. She had no car to insure and no land to build a house on. Caleb had both and was fighting to keep them.

He started toward the house and she followed. His phone buzzed. When he glanced at the screen a puff of air blew out of his mouth and the corner of his lips hitched up. "Guess Justin isn't coming home tonight. He asked if I could do chores in the morning."

"What? No. I can do them. You have your own ranch's chores. Why wouldn't he have asked me?" Her phone had been silent all night. Its typical state.

"Probably because he didn't want to ask his adult sister to cover for him while he's getting laid."

She choked on a gasp, partly from being scandalized and partly because sucking in that much cold air was a shock to her throat.

Caleb's deep chuckle prompted a smile from her. A smiling Caleb was always better.

Inside, he shucked his boots off. "I'll take his bathroom. I'm sure he'd rather have me bear witness to anything embarrassing than you."

"I would argue, but I don't want to find out what he might have that's incriminating. I'm just glad he didn't bring his hookup here."

"You're not the only one." He tossed his hat onto a hook and sauntered off, running a hand through his hair. Her fingers itched to do it for him.

She finished toeing her boots off, watching him disappear into the master bedroom from under the brim of her own hat. Even barefoot, the guy had an unmistakable swagger. When they'd been kids, he'd never quit moving, bouncing around with energy. Poking at her or her brother until he got a reaction. Always laughing and joking.

Now, his energy was coiled. She still spied that boy she once knew. Good-natured, a touch wild, but with a ready smile.

God, she had missed him.

She could just add that feeling to the nostalgia that liked to broadside her at unexpected times now that she was home. There was a lot about her home that she'd missed. Her hometown? Not so much.

She jogged up the stairs and darted into the bathroom. The door clicked shut and she glanced at the empty hook on the back of the door. Stripping down, she caught sight of herself in the mirror.

And there it was. The reason she'd thrown a small shit fit when Oliver had insisted on moving back. She stared at herself in the mirror, at the boobs she had a hard time containing. Now that she'd gained some weight, they threatened to spill out of her bra. How could she be a damn adult and still be plagued by childhood insecurities?

Maisy May Jorgenson and her incessant need to point out that Brigit's sports bra got an F in containment. Or Maisy's best friend, Priya Patel, quietly whispering in Brigit's ear that her gym shorts rode up when she bent over. Priya had acted like what she'd done was in Brigit's best interest, but from the smug look on Maisy's face, that was doubtful.

Brigit sneered and flipped the lever to the shower with more force than she intended. Water burst on, splashing over the tub ledge onto the fluffy charcoal gray bathmat and beyond.

Dammit, she'd have to clean that up. But for now, she had to scrub the grit off and hope her memories went down the drain with it. She freed her hair and stepped under the spray, shivering until it warmed.

High school for a girl with growth spurts like hers hadn't been fun. Those tight gym shorts? They'd been long and loose when school let out her sophomore year. Over the next summer, Brigit had grown three inches and developed curves that had made her seem wider *and* taller than everyone else. The adult part of her saw her classmates' behavior for what it was. Jealousy. Insecurity. Intimidation. Mean-girl tactics used to make themselves feel better.

Junior year, Brigit hadn't lacked for homecoming dates, and for prom that year, she'd even gone with Maisy's brother, who had been a senior. That'd been out of spite. And because Mom had refused to allow her to go with Caleb.

But I'd be more comfortable going with a friend. Though, she hadn't been eying Caleb with a friend's eyes. By then, he'd done his own growing, getting taller than her and developing those muscles. Those muscles. Their work today and through the night wasn't sexy, but it'd been with him. All day. All that bending and flexing, and that ass…

All chill fled as she remembered Caleb's sure movements. She'd only seen adult him in a shirt and pants, but—

Enough. No thoughts of shirtless Caleb Cruise while she showered.

She rinsed and flipped the water off. Stepping out, she grabbed a towel and dried off while staring at the door. All she had were dirty clothes. She couldn't hear footsteps or any other sound to indicate Caleb had finished his shower, though he had to be done by now.

The towel wrapped far enough around her to be secure. It'd be nice if Justin bought a color other than pewter gray, but there was no one around to see how ashen it made her look. She brushed out her hair and bypassed the noisy hair dryer. She'd take care of that in her room.

She whipped open the door and pulled up short. The water on the floor. Spinning, she yanked the hand towel off the ring by the light switch and carefully bent to mop up the water.

Lobbing the hand towel toward the laundry bin, she turned. Her breath caught.

Whatever she'd thought about a shirtless Caleb didn't come close to the real thing.

He was stopped in the hallway, like he'd seen her crouched in nothing but a towel and gotten glued to the spot. A matching gray towel was slung low over his waist, the rest of his lean body bare.

And wow.

Defined pecs. Rippling abs she wanted to gaze at as much as she wanted to trace with her tongue. There was nothing relaxed about him. This wasn't the usual Caleb.

Because they were both wearing only a towel. Her gaze flew to his face, but his was stuck on the flare of her hips. His jaw tightened until she thought he'd bust teeth. He finally noticed her looking at him.

"Fuck, sorry." He stiffly turned his head, like he'd defaulted to robot mode.

"Yeah." She wasn't sorry. There wasn't any more chance she and Caleb would work than there had been ten years ago.

Might as well torture herself with what she was missing. That view was worth it.

She took a step, her heel hitting a patch that hadn't completely dried, which had turned into an ice rink for the unwary. The skid of her foot on the ceramic tile was louder than her startled cry. Her biggest worry wasn't that she'd hurt herself. It was that she'd crash to the ground and lose her towel, or land with her legs splayed in the unsexiest peep show to ever hit Moore, Minnesota.

Her other foot hit with a thud and she caught herself. The pounding of her heart clogged her throat and she put a hand to her chest.

Caleb was at her side, a sexy safety net she would've gratefully fallen into. "Are you all right?" His hot hand was on her elbow. He was only inches away from her.

"You move fast." She blinked and tried to lift her gaze to his face, but it was glued to the way his muscles flowed from his shoulders to his chest.

He dropped his voice. "Not when it counts, honey."

He'd meant it as a joke, she knew that. But the timbre of his drawl and the proximity of his nearly naked body belied the humor. She couldn't get past her raw need. How did the adult Caleb feel? Would he still like when she nibbled along his jawline to his earlobe? Would he groan every time she stroked his length?

She swallowed hard. Somehow, he'd crowded closer. Or had she drawn nearer?

Who cared?

"Bridge." His voice matched the raging hormones inside of hers, the ones demanding answers to her questions.

She lifted her chin and kissed the corner of his mouth and pulled back only slightly. "Caleb."

"We shouldn't—"

"I know." She planted her lips on his.

His reaction was immediate. Her back hit the wall as his body pressed against hers. She wrapped her arms around him and deepened the kiss. His taste was achingly familiar, one that promised to fill the empty chasm inside of her.

When his tongue stroked inside her mouth, she greedily received him. The delicious press of his growing erection between them made her curse her towel. She should have let it fall when she slipped.

His hands gripped her ass, bringing her closer. She skimmed her hands up to his face, loving the rough scrape of his stubble against her palms and the slide of silky wet hair over her heated skin.

She rolled her hips, reveling in the steel trapped between them. Everything was bigger about Caleb.

His groan resonated through his chest into hers. She rolled against him again, only this time she sought desperate relief for the throbbing ache between her legs. Releasing his head, she gripped his shoulders. Should she wrap a leg around him? Maybe widen her stance so they could rock together? Or palm him and give him at least the same measure of ecstasy she was feeling?

He ripped his mouth free and rested his forehead against hers, his breathing heavy. "We can't do this."

"I know," she breathed. Why again?

"You said that before and now my dick is hard as a rock." He let go of her butt, moving his hands to her arms.

"It's harder."

The intensity of his dark gaze speared her, but he recovered. "You're not helping."

She sighed and cupped his face. "Look, I know we have a history, and I should've gone about breaking up with you better. And I know your roots are here and here is where you're going to stay."

"And there's no way you'd settle in Moore with a guy like me."

She frowned and slid her hands to his shoulders. Not touching him while they were this close wasn't an option. "It's not you, it's Moore."

He let her go and stepped back, glancing down like he was making sure he was still covered. The loss of his heat let the chill flow in like a rushing river. Goose bumps crawled over her arms. She twisted her hands into her towel, but not to hold it up. Her earlier vulnerability was exposed for all to see now.

"If it's not me, why couldn't we tell anyone about us back then? I was prouder than hell of dating a girl like you."

Her heart melted at the same time it cracked with heartbreak. He thought she was ashamed of him? *She* wasn't. Her mom was a different story. "If anyone had found out, it would have gotten back to Mom. And you know how she is."

"Anti me."

Brigit nodded. "I didn't want to ruin my chance at being with you."

"And when your mom found out? We were done, easy as that?"

She stiffened, clutching the hem of the towel harder. "It wasn't *easy*. I..." She'd loved him. With all the strength of a seventeen-year-old in love for the first time in her life. "I didn't trust myself around you. But like Mom pointed out, we were going different directions and there was no way in hell I was staying here."

He retreated farther, sweeping his mussed hair off his face as he brushed his gaze over her. She shifted her weight. Did he still like what he saw? She'd been curvy like this when they were together, yet no one since had made her feel as sexy as he had.

"I guess we're back there again. I'm not leaving. You're

not staying. And your mom would still throw a shit fit if she found out I'd touched you."

She didn't want to agree, but her head seemed to nod of its own accord. If the reason they couldn't be together was so simple, why was it so hard to remember?

CHAPTER 7

"That's the estimate for a new hood. Add that to the new fender and touching up the paint..." The auto shop employee rattled off numbers that were only rivaled in size by the guy's booming voice.

Caleb threaded steel into his spine to keep from sinking back into the hard-plastic seat of the waiting room and dropping his head into his hands. He'd never thought the body shop such a depressing place before.

A sheet of paper hung from Larry's black-smudged fingers. Caleb didn't want to accept the estimate. He had an emergency fund but it wasn't big enough to cover this. That meant he'd have to dig into the insurance payout from his house.

Larry was waiting.

"How long will the repairs take?" He had an old pickup that he kept running, so a backup wasn't an issue. The time without his regular ride just added to the general inconvenience of it all.

"About a week. But we can't fit you in until next week." Larry shrugged a heavy shoulder. "It's drivable."

Yeah, if he wanted to go back to cruising around in a beater that people would use to judge his character. That'd worked so well for him in high school.

"Go ahead and write me in. I'll drop it off Monday before work." He'd figure out how to get home from work Tuesday morning.

Larry still held the paper. A bushy eyebrow rose and he jiggled it.

No, Caleb didn't want to take proof of how much less he had for a house. His policy was going to increase after this claim.

He found where Larry had parked his pickup outside the shop. A brisk wind cut through his sweater. His heavier winter coat was draped across his backseat, where it was nice and warm. He crawled inside and blew out a breath. The cold was refreshing, and he needed it to keep his head from returning to that steamy bathroom with a not-naked-enough Brigit.

He'd had her in his arms again. Her round ass in his hands. Her tongue in his mouth.

And she'd responded with as much energy as he had. If he hadn't forced himself to stop, would he have been inside her? Would either of them have thought about protection?

Would he have cared?

Yes, of course. He'd been safe his whole sex life, and someday he'd love to be a dad, but only if the other person was all in. Brigit had never mentioned kids. Maybe once, and only as a rigid step in her ideal life path. College. Career. Marriage. Kids. And none of that shit in Moore.

So he should pat himself on the back. His restraint had been Herculean. If only he could stop imagining how it might've felt to have nothing between them—both literally and metaphorically.

He flung the pickup into gear, not knowing where he was going and not caring.

The morning had been spent on the phone with his insurance agent while he finished chores. He'd missed lunch while he waited for the estimate on his vehicle.

His stomach rumbled. Okay, then. Food. He might as well run through the grocery store. But first the butcher shop. The deer wasn't going to squeeze itself into sausage casings.

He was across town within minutes. Walking into the butcher shop, he nearly groaned. The scent of spices surrounded him, reminding him of their meat-filled dinner with the Jameses. Just what he needed. Another Brigit recollection rising up like the lady of the lake. Hanging out last night. Being together. In public—sort of. It might've been as friends, but he hadn't realized how badly he'd wanted that. No matter how many years had passed, he went back to being that kid who yearned to be out with his girlfriend.

As he wound around the shelves full of seasonings and marinades, another smell hit him. Flowery perfume that clashed with the savory scents.

"Caleb?"

He turned toward the unfamiliar female voice. It took a moment to recognize the girl he'd gone to school with. Priya Patel had grown into some dead-sexy curves. Long, shiny black hair hung over one shoulder, but the biggest change was the lighter touch she wielded with her makeup brush. Her natural beauty had a chance to shine through.

The first smile of the day hit him. "Priya, hey. Back in town?"

They hadn't hung out in the same crowd until her best friend had dated Justin. Then broken up with him. Then dated him again. Maisy wasn't on the list of people he missed socializing with, but seeing Priya again was nice. She'd always balanced the effect of Maisy.

Why couldn't he have been interested in Priya? She probably harbored feelings for Justin, but still. How would things have been different? Instead, he'd given his heart to one woman.

And moved on. Sort of. He dated other women, had sporadic sex, and tried not to think about growing old alone.

Priya grinned and crossed her arms, the mass of necklaces around her neck jingling. "I'm actually back for good."

"Seriously?" He glanced around. The owner of the shop nodded at him from behind the counter. That's right. Priya's grandpa ran the place.

"Yeah. I'm finishing my residency and I got a position here." She spread her hands out. "Meet the new OB/GYN in town."

"Hey, congrats."

"Thanks. And you? I've been so far in the med school rabbit hole, I haven't heard much, except from, you know. Maisy." Her smile turned strained. Apparently, the relationship between him and Brigit wasn't the only one to suffer under maturity.

"I'm a fireman."

Her laugh tinkled through the shop. "Of course. How could I forget that was your dream job? Didn't your family ranch like Justin's?"

"Yep. I do both."

"A fireman rancher. Awesome."

"That's me." He got that a lot, but at least Priya wasn't oozing shock and awe. He got that a lot, too, from people he used to know. *Look at Caleb Cruise. He actually did something with himself.*

Her laugh was as beautiful as she was, but he'd never been drawn into the mob of boys drooling after Priya Patel. Like Brigit, she'd left home for education and success. But she was back to stay. Only she wasn't staying under the same roof.

And he hadn't made out with her wearing nothing but a towel less than twelve hours ago.

Not only that, but Priya didn't stop him in his tracks like Brigit did crouched in that damn towel. His mouth didn't dry up and his entire blood supply didn't rush to his groin despite being only feet away from her. Sure, Priya's grandpa was close by and they were in public.

But when Brigit was around, it didn't matter. And since she was still in Moore, and under Justin's roof, and single, he'd have to hold his shit together. He'd been single this long. He'd used his hand so much that he didn't have to worry about wasting water in the shower. Going without sex to keep from doing something stupid and creating a shit-ton of drama in his life wasn't that hard.

"Is your grandpa busy?" Talking to an old friend shouldn't be so depressing.

"Grandpa Saunders is always busy. But he's always got time for his customers." She moved back to let him pass. "I'm sure we'll cross paths anyway if Maisy's seeing Justin again."

That was enough to pull him to a stop. Justin's life was none of his business, but Maisy getting close to Brigit's brother was enough to raise alarms. Maisy wasn't any nicer now than she'd been in high school, and she hadn't set the bar high.

Maisy was the type of girl who put down others to feel better about herself. She could also charm whoever she was talking to as she was stabbing them in the back. Brigit had never confessed to how badly she'd been targeted, but Caleb had read the signs. The red eyes after gym class. The hunched shoulders and averted gaze as Maisy and her cohorts sauntered by. The avoidance of any school function run by the cheerleaders. Their team captain at the time: Maisy.

But she was hot and single. And must've fooled Justin

enough to tap back into his high school on-again off-again girlfriend and all the drama she fostered.

Even Joan Walker had sensed something off about that girl. Maisy had never been allowed at the house. Brigit had either talked to her mother, or Joan had read the mean-girl vibes loud and clear.

That was one thing they could agree on.

He left her with a "see you around" and found her grandfather.

As he made arrangements for processing the deer, his mind puzzled over the Maisy question. Would she be the wedge that permanently drove Brigit from her home?

It smelled like snow. Brigit stamped the fresh straw under her feet. She was in the barn with Justin, pitching in to clean the muck left behind by a couple of sick sheep they'd been doctoring.

"Mom and Dad are coming for Thanksgiving next week," Justin announced with all the delicacy of a charging ram.

She didn't bother hiding her groan. One thing she and her twin commiserated over was parental pushiness. Justin couldn't dodge it now that he'd come back home. Neither could she.

"How long and where are they staying?" Her thoughts turned to Caleb. What was he going to do?

"I told them there was still a bedroom left. Mom said she'd get back to me."

"She's going to comment about how it'll be crowded with Caleb taking a room." Somehow, the barn was their safe space. It had always been where they teamed up to bitch about Mom and Dad's interference. In the house, they passed each other like there was a fence between them. He did his thing, she did hers.

But the barn. Surrounded by the familiar scent of manure, straw, and musty dirt, they dropped their guards. Maybe it was because they'd spent their childhoods outside.

Justin grunted and unhooked a corral panel that had been separating the sheep. "I already told her that he was my guest. I even listed how he contributed."

For Justin to go that far in explaining his life? Mom would know not to push the Caleb subject.

He pushed the brim of his ball cap up. She always teased him that his cowboy hat was just for show. When he ranched, he wore an old grungy ball cap. "I never understood what she had against him."

Mom held Caleb's allure against him. Brigit and Justin and Caleb had been close, but Justin hadn't been the one to entertain skipping college to live with Caleb. After the fight with Dad about letting Brigit go where she wanted for school and getting treated the same as the boys, for Brigit, Caleb was a huge threat. But for Justin, Mom only held Caleb's family against him. "She was afraid her precious Justin would be corrupted by a student with less than a four-point-oh GPA."

"Right? I almost wish I still had a reason to go to Denver for the holiday." He clenched his jaw and looked away.

Brigit didn't have to ask for specifics. That Justin had mentioned even this much meant the situation was gnawing at him. "She really did a number on you, huh?"

"How long can one guy try before he gives up?" A disgusted sound ripped out of him. "Until she gets engaged to someone else, I guess."

She blinked and looked away. His question propelled her back to the scene in the bathroom. Caleb was still trying to give up. She hadn't encouraged him to. Instead, she'd practically scaled his body, made herself his hood ornament. But this moment wasn't about her pain and insecurities. "She wasn't the one, I guess."

"Guess not." He shrugged and kicked at a pile of straw. "At least Maisy doesn't cross her signals."

Cold shock washed down her spine. "Maisy May?" Justin's expression turned sheepish. She couldn't believe he'd be so stupid. "What were you thinking? She's gonna be here one day boiling a bunny on our stove," she hissed.

"She's not that crazy. And have you ever seen that movie?"

She had. And she'd thought of Maisy at the time. "Guys have a blind spot forty-acres wide when it comes to crazy women. It's like you get more attracted to them." She shook her head. "She's a mean one."

"How would you know? You didn't even hang out with her."

"For good reason."

"Whatever. That was years ago. And she never said anything bad about you."

Her snort echoed through the barn. "As if she'd trash your twin to you and expect you to keep going out with her."

"Well, it's not serious and she knows that."

Brigit wasn't so sure. "Watch yourself. She's got more than one personality and you only see the sane one."

"Noted." His back was to her as he stacked corral panels.

He was brushing her advice off that easily? Did it not bother him that Maisy was her own personal bully? "What's noted is the door you just slammed closed."

"Want to talk about doors?" He turned around and crossed his arms. "Why are you and Caleb acting like complete strangers?"

"I— What?" She looked around for something to do. Anything.

"Do you think I missed the whole drama between you

and him? And how he always gets tense when you're around but seems to look for you everywhere? And how now that you're both under the same roof, you aren't talking to each other even though we all used to ride horse together, build forts in the shelter belts, and work cattle as a team?"

"I helped him work cattle all last weekend. While you were doing business." It might've been a touch coldhearted to point that out, since his *business* hadn't gone so well, but she really didn't want to talk about Caleb to Justin.

But he ignored the jab. "So you two should be laughing and joking around. Especially after field dressing a deer together."

Brigit wanted to rub her forehead, but her hands were dirty. "Mom didn't approve."

"We covered that. So?"

"She lost her shit when she caught us together."

Justin's blue eyes went wide. "Like, *together* together?"

"I thought you said you didn't miss the drama between us."

"I didn't miss that you two went from sneaking looks and whispering in dark corners to not talking—at all."

Well, damn. She'd spilled stale beans that were best left covered. "So he never said anything?"

"About you? Never."

Brigit looked down, inspecting the toe of her boot. "We thought you'd be mad."

"Because my best friend wanted my sister? Why? He's a good guy. One of the best."

He spoke like it was such a given. And it was. But whether Caleb was a decent man or not had never been an issue in her mind. "We want different things."

"But you want each other?"

"Right. So it's easier to keep our distance."

Justin shook his head and grabbed his worn sheepskin

jacket from where it was hanging. He shrugged into it. "What's your deal against Moore anyway?"

Like Caleb, Justin didn't understand. "There's nothing here for me."

"Other than Caleb."

She rolled her eyes. "Right. I stay here and make babies and get married and forget the whole career thing."

"No one's expecting you to do that. Staying in Moore doesn't mean you're condemned to maternal servitude." He peered at her. "I didn't realize you were so against the whole family thing."

"I'm not." She sounded sullen, but the truth was she wanted a family of her own more than anything. But she wanted a career she could be proud of, too, and she wanted to do that first. The years were ticking away, and she was losing her chance at both of them. Her brothers had been able to go school and come back and have a ranching career handed to them. "I just want to have something of my own."

Understanding flashed through his eyes. He wasn't technically the youngest, but like her, he'd watched their older brother and the other firstborn cousins become the pride and joy of the Walker family. She and Justin had been told to be relieved. Dad claimed they should be grateful that the responsibility hadn't fallen on them. *It's a big operation. A lot of people depending on you and too many variables out of your control.* But no one understood the lingering feeling of *What now?* Where was their place in the world if not their own home?

He nodded. "Yeah, I get that. Law school not working out really threw you for a loop."

"Yeah." She almost winced. Did she sound as taken off guard as she felt? She almost never thought about law school. That ship had sailed—after she'd untied the rope and pushed it out to sea. But no one knew that. "I'm still trying to figure out what I want to be when I grow up. Oliver was a huge setback. I almost settled with a guy who would've glued my feet to the kitchen floor and blamed me for buying the glue."

"I've been meaning to ask you 'what the hell' about Oliver, but I thought it was too soon."

"Maisy May Jorgenson," she said flatly.

"Like I said—"

She barked out a laugh. "Talk to me again in a year and we'll see how that turned out. Anyway, I have no land and no house, and the only job openings in town barely pay above minimum wage or need a specialized degree I don't have."

"I get that." Justin started for the house. "So here's the deal. You gotta help me clean the house so Mom doesn't get here and run her finger over the mantel again."

She chuckled and said in a prim tone, "'Oh, I do hope this house holds up through your bachelor years.'"

Justin's laugh sent her back to their childhood, when they'd do chores and get into deep discussions about life. "As if my future wife is going to clean up after my ass. And I dust at least once a month."

"Mom used to dust daily. And she ironed our jeans." They lobbed house-cleaning memories back and forth and Brigit had never been so grateful. It didn't keep one particular question from cycling in her head.

Caleb would want to avoid her mom during the holidays. He wasn't a guy who wanted to cause tension. But with no house and no family, where would he go on Thanksgiving?

CHAPTER 8

This still wasn't his worst Thanksgiving ever. That award went to the year he was in kindergarten. All he'd understood then was that he had a long break from school and he was hungry.

Mom had just met Russ and was wildly happy, or just wild. So was Russ. The man was nice enough to Caleb. Nicer than any of her previous boyfriends. That wasn't why Caleb called him Dad.

No, he did that to blend in. Nearly all the other kids at school had a mom and a dad, divorced or not. It only took explaining once that he didn't know who his dad was to teach him never to admit that again.

That year, Mom tossed a frozen turkey into the oven, trying to impress Russ with cooking skills she didn't possess. If it weren't for beef stew dumped out of a can and Kraft mac and cheese, Caleb would've starved before the first hot lunch at school. And he wouldn't have eaten at school if Grandma hadn't kept that account current.

The turkey took hours to cook and by then, his parents had consumed every drop of alcohol in the house and passed out. Caleb knew enough to turn the oven off before going to bed with stomach cramps so severe he hadn't slept all night.

The entire day had sucked. No cable. No phone available to him. Too cold to play outside. He'd sat inside all day and driven his little Matchbox car through every room. He'd used wadded-up socks as cattle and played rancher. And he'd rushed around with an imaginary hose, putting out fires.

Quietly, of course. Bothering Mom when she was drinking and cuddling Russ never ended well.

The rest of the weekend he'd spent at Grandma's, where he'd stuffed himself until he puked.

The crinkle of the gas station sandwich wrapper was the only sound in the motel room. He inspected the limp bun and the meat patty that maybe had some actual beef in it. It was covered in manufactured cheese product, but Caleb doubted actual milk had made it onto the ingredient list.

The motel room could've been worse. There was a lot of room for improvement, but guests didn't stay at the Moore-tel for comfort. It was little more than a stopping point for hunters. A fish-cleaning station was parked at the end of the building and there was a sign posted in probably every bath-room exhorting guests not to clean fowl in the shower. Too many hunters thought it was a great idea to just clean their birds in the shitter.

He took a bite of his burger and grimaced. Between the gas station where he'd heated it and the two-minute ride back—and the few minutes he'd allowed himself a little pity party—his food had cooled. He couldn't stomach cold pseudomeat.

Funny, at one point in his life, he would've hoovered anything edible and attempted a few things that weren't. He'd gotten soft.

Tossing the burger in the bag, he grabbed an apple from

the cooler he'd packed from Justin's. Clearing out before Rick and Joan arrived had been a priority.

He'd tried switching shifts, but the guys on duty didn't want to lose the holiday pay. Couldn't blame them. He was scheduled to work Christmas and he'd gladly pick up another holiday for the money. His good pickup was in the shop, and while it didn't have great gas mileage, his current forty-year-old truck ate gas like it was a starving five-year-old left to his own devices on Thanksgiving.

Look at that. He was back at the pity party again.

The apple wasn't nearly as satisfying but the kick of sweetness brightened the five minutes it took to eat it. If the grocery store were open, he'd buy something more substantial—that didn't need heating or refrigeration, of course. This wasn't one of those kinds of rooms.

With a sigh, he tossed the core in the garbage on top of his uneaten burger. Ain't that a picture for the Christmas card.

A dot of sweat popped on his forehead. He'd turned the heat down after check-in but it was like he had his own in-room bonfire churning. The sweater he'd worn here was already draped over the back of the rickety chair by the coatrack. He shrugged out of his shirt. Guess he wouldn't need to go out and get his winter coat after all. After he'd dumped his duffel in the room and felt how thin the comforter was, he'd considered gathering every spare scrap of material he had to use as blankets.

But at this rate, he was going to have to sleep with the windows open.

Flipping on the TV, he scanned through the channels.

"Fuck me." Three channels and only one came in decently. And here he was without his Matchbox car.

He sprawled across the top of the bed, spreading out his body to keep from trapping heat in.

What would the Walkers be doing? He'd subtly asked Jesse what their plans were. His sister had invited Jesse, Farah, and her parents over. If it'd been the other way around, he would've casually invited himself over, but he wasn't low enough to invite himself over to another Walker's.

So he'd played casual with Justin, said it was no problem, that he'd get a room and give Justin's family space. They were good enough friends that Justin didn't push it and dent his pride.

But, man, this sucked.

THE MEAL WAS OVER. Brigit stacked dishes in the dishwasher, her patience balancing on a razor's edge. She should be stuffed, but Mom had thought one pie for just the four of them was enough. Not only that, half the damn pumpkin pie was left.

She slammed a plate into the slot.

Someone entered the kitchen behind her. Was she lucky enough that it was Justin?

"I definitely think brining is the way to go next time," Mom said. "Then the turkey won't get so dry."

The turkey had been only a little dry. "That's what gravy's for."

"Better to eat turkey, not liquid fat."

Gravy was broth and flour and bullion—and a little grease for flavor. But whatever.

Mom positioned herself at the sink behind Brigit to rinse off plates before they went into the dishwasher. Which Brigit never did. Because they had a dishwasher.

"This was a cozy holiday between us." Mom sighed wistfully. "I miss Travis and the kids."

Brigit lifted a brow. "And Kami."

Travis's wife had once been on the same level as Caleb in Mom's opinion. Mom liked her well enough now, but it was still "Travis and the kids." Like she couldn't help her fiercely protective streak around her kids.

"Oh, of course." Mom slid in an as-good-as-clean plate toward her. "Funny how we used to have these gigantic gatherings and now we're all divided up. Cash and Abbi went to her family's. Dillon and Elle had her dad out." She chuckled. "Aaron said he was getting a decoy turkey to keep his brothers away from all the dark meat, and Brock had his in-laws over—all of them, I guess. Never thought I'd see the day he'd entertain so many people in his home."

Brigit was nodding, mildly interested. Her cousins all had their own families and she didn't see them much outside of planting, harvesting, and working cattle. But Mom's last words dawned on her. *All* Brock's in-laws.

"Farah's parents went to Brock's too?" She'd assumed Caleb would head over to the Jameses for the day.

"I guess." Mom slid another cleaned, dripping plate over.

"I wonder what Caleb did today." She hadn't meant to say that out loud. Maybe she had. To make a point.

"I'm sure he found something to do."

Brigit stopped loading. With who? Had one of his fireman buddies invited him over? Or was he alone?

Mom was too busy rinsing dishes to notice her reaction. "It's a good thing, really, that he chose to go to a motel. I don't get much time with just you and Justin."

"He's been friends with Justin for, like, twenty years. Most families would welcome him at their table."

Mom tapped the lever down, shutting the water off. "Caleb has impressed me with how well he's done for himself." Brigit tensed as Mom caught her gaze and held it. "But considering your past, and what you're getting over, it's best if he keeps his distance."

"Even if his distance means he spends Thanksgiving by himself, alone in a motel room because his home was trashed?"

"How do you know he's alone?"

Brigit drew back. Anger curled inside of her, faintly at first, like a cow lowing in a far-off pasture, then swelling larger, like a full-on stampede. Was it just her mother's casual reaction that was fueling the feeling, or was it the idea that Caleb might have sought out companionship when he felt like everyone had forgotten him?

"I didn't mean it like that, Brigit. His life is in Moore. Justin isn't his only friend."

No, but Caleb had no family around today. Brigit broke eye contact when she stooped to grab the dishwasher detergent. Without a word, she dropped the tab of dried soap into its slot and used her toe to flip the lid closed.

"I guess I'll find out when I bring him a plate of food." She didn't wait for Mom's reaction as she collected a plate and silverware. Mom didn't move as she dug out the leftovers that had been neatly packed away.

"What if he's already had a big meal?" Mom hadn't moved, but she clocked Brigit's every movement. No doubt she was racking her brain, trying to come up with a good reason to keep her own daughter from showing a guy with no family some compassion on a holiday. Even if that guy was the biggest threat to said daughter's nonexistent career.

"There was nothing open today. Even the bars are closed." Brigit heaped potatoes onto a plate with turkey and stuffing. Topped by gravy. She had no idea if Caleb liked white meat or dark meat, gravy on top or on the side or not at all, or if he cared that there wasn't a single vegetable in sight. She didn't know his preferences at all.

A spike of irritation was taken out on the spoon as she splattered gravy on the counter.

Ignoring the mess, she covered the food with plastic wrap and hefted the plate. It had to weigh a few pounds. "I don't know when I'll be back."

She charged out of the kitchen, passing the counter that held the remains of the pie. Hesitating for a second, she snagged the dish in her other hand.

"The pie…" Mom's protest faded as Brigit walked away. Justin reclined with Dad in front of the TV, his brows popping when he saw her load and her trajectory straight for the door. His gaze lifted beyond her to where Mom must be wringing her hands. He kicked the footrest down and sat up.

Dad barely spared her a glance and it was back to the game.

There was no good way to set her items down and get her shoes on, so she stomped her feet into each boot. The tops pushed her jeans up her legs, but she didn't care. She managed to juggle the dishes in one arm and grab her coat.

Then she was out the door, her Mom's call of "Brigit" dissipating in the cold air.

She stomped down the steps and as soon as her shoes hit the dirt, she clenched her teeth. "Dammit."

She had no vehicle. After her dramatic little exit, she couldn't very well go inside and ask Dad to borrow the car.

The screen door squeaked open and a set of keys jingled. She looked back. Justin was grinning as he came to a stop on the last stair.

Her relieved smile had to take up half her face. "Thank you."

"Moore-tel."

She knew, but the extra show of support warmed her. He jogged back inside, probably for a night of tight-lipped glaring from Mom, but he would handle it better. Brigit had already endured an interrogation over where she had applied for jobs, what cities she was looking at, why law school was out of the question, and if she'd talked to Oliver. All before she'd been told she shouldn't have seconds on pie.

On the way into town, her heart rate kicked up instead of slowing down. This didn't mean anything. It was just bringing dinner to a friend.

Was Caleb even a friend? Lord knew, she'd pushed him far enough away she could see why she questioned herself.

The motel's parking lot was lit, and Caleb's old beater pickup was parked in front of room four. She pulled in next to him and killed the engine. Her stomach flipped as she stared at the blue door.

Well, she'd come this far. It'd be cruel to chicken out now and drive away with all the food. Not that Caleb knew she was coming.

Sliding out, she winced as the freezing air hit her face. Her pants were gathered in a messy bunch over her cowboy boots, and she wore the same long-sleeved V-neck purple shirt she'd had on all day. Not fancy, but not pajamas. And not a towel.

A punch of heat warded off the chill. She steeled herself, gathered the food, and marched to the door. She kicked at it in place of knocking.

Two seconds later, the door opened a crack, a chain breaking Caleb's face in two.

Surprise, then concern, flashed over his features. "Brigit. Everything okay?"

She pushed for a smile and held the plates up. "I assumed you'd be hanging out with Farah today, but I heard they went to Brock's. So…"

The door closed, but the rattle of the chain was crystal clear. Then he whipped open the door and ushered her in.

"Holy crap, it's hot in here." If she'd been wearing her coat, she would've started sweating.

Caleb locked the door and circled around her. Her mouth went dry.

He was shirtless.

His hair wasn't slicked from his shower this time and his jeans were on, but the effect packed no less punch than last time.

"I legit think I have to open a window. I've turned the heat off, but there's no circulation in here and I think the owner cranked the thermostat in the neighboring rooms." He accepted the plates and set them down. She stepped out of her boots, not bothering to ask if she was welcome to stay.

"I think you could leave the door wide open and it might drop below eighty in an hour." She went to the window on the opposite side of the door and cracked it. The blast of wind should help take the flush out of her face.

Caleb waved at all the food. "Is this… Thanks."

"No problem." And it wasn't. He was staring at the food like it was a feast for kings. This was worth whatever fallout happened at home. "It hasn't been in the fridge long, but it might need a quick reheat."

A scan of the room said no, that wouldn't be an option.

Caleb chuckled. "Believe me, it's better than the apple I had."

"Is that all you've eaten?"

"And a gas station burger." His gaze strayed to the garbage can next to her.

She looked down. "Ah. At least I remembered a fork."

"Just one? Aren't you going to join me?" He tossed his jacket off a chair and carried the seat to the bed. To her dismay, he found his shirt and rolled it on. "Take your pick while I bring the table over."

She settled on the uncomfortable chair and he took the bed. He shoveled into the potatoes with one hand while lifting the foil cover off the pie. "Half a pie. Damn."

"I know it's too much." She couldn't explain the situation without hurting his feelings. He didn't need to deal with her mom's opinions on top of…well, hers. "I wasn't sure what you like, or how you like it."

"Now I didn't say it was too much." He scooted the pie tray over. "Half is yours."

Her mouth watered. Pumpkin pie was her favorite. "I should've packed another fork."

He shrugged and finished chewing his mouthful, another forkful poised and ready. "Use your hands."

Her smile had a mind of its own. "I can't eat pumpkin pie with my hands."

He winked. "Betcha you could." He held the handle of his fork. "But if you're too scared, you use the fork and I'll use my hands on these potatoes."

She scowled at him and grabbed the pie pan, strategizing how to manage without wearing half the pumpkin custard.

His grin was unrepentant and he went back to his food. Once she loosened her piece, the rest was pretty easy to eat. She polished off a slice.

Caleb tapped the tin. "I'm not done yet. Might as well have another."

She wiped her hands down her jeans, liking their makeshift picnic. "I'd better not."

"Full?"

"I can always eat pie." She held her breath for a moment, then let the words spill out. "You know why there was half a one left? Mom suggested we save it for tomorrow. After she commented that I might have to buy a new wardrobe. Black Friday deals and all."

Caleb's fork hung from his hand and he had a *you're shitting me* look. He set the utensil down. "The only problem with your weight is the people who comment on it."

"I wish it were that clear-cut."

He stared at her for a heartbeat. "I was going to say something like 'it could be that clear-cut,' but I'm not a girl."

The corner of her mouth hitched up, and the flush came back as she recalled him with his shirt off. "No. Definitely not a girl."

"I like the way you look. I've always liked the way you look. And I think you look better now than ever." He shook his head as a shadow crossed his face. "This thing with your mom. She has some baggage that she's been handing off to you. The perfectionism, the way she lives vicariously through you, the weird shit about your eating. It's not right, and it's about her and not you."

Brigit folded her hands in her lap. She couldn't nod, but he was right. It wasn't like she couldn't see it. What she couldn't see was that her mom was incorrect. "The thing about Mom is... she's right sometimes. Her nagging about my career? She was there when I came home from high school and finally broke down. I was such an outsider. Taller than the rest of my classmates, even after they hit puberty. Justin was the popular one, not me."

"I didn't realize it was so bad."

"You were Justin's friend and had a little cult following you were oblivious to. When I moved for college—" Her voice cracked. Those days were the epitome of bittersweet. "Mom and I went shopping. New town, new look. It was... exhilarating freedom." Brigit shifted her gaze to the wall. The flash of hurt in Caleb's eyes inspired a new round of guilt. "I walked into the grocery store and no one knew who I was. No one commented on my clothing. No one compared me to my brothers. The anonymity was addicting."

"And your mom knew what waited for you."

She nodded. Mom had had the same experience in a different small town. Things should be different now that

Brigit was an adult. But nothing had changed. "Did you know Justin's seeing Maisy again?"

"Priya mentioned it last week when I saw her."

Priya was back in town? And Caleb had talked to her? That wasn't jealousy piercing her gut and churning the dessert she'd eaten. Who Caleb dated wasn't her business.

"Relax. I think Priya would go after Justin if she thought she'd survive Maisy's assassination attempts."

Her tension faded. "I wish Justin weren't rebelling against the woman who broke his heart. I wish he had a thing for Priya instead."

His dark eyes twinkled. "I seem to have a thing for tall blonds who can work cattle like a boss and keep trying to get away from me."

"It's not you I'm getting away from." Being close to him made her question what was so important that she had to leave Moore and him behind. The longer she was around him, the more the answer faded away.

His nod was curt. "Fair enough."

CHAPTER 9

$\mathcal{I}$f someone had asked him this morning whether he'd be stretched out next to Brigit Walker on his motel bed, he would've laughed, then tormented himself with the fantasy.

Now if they'd told him he'd be fully clothed and so would she and they'd both be on top of the covers, well, that was in the realm of believability.

"If you could be anything you wanted to be when you grow up, what would it be?" he asked, turning his head. Brigit was staring at the drop-tile ceiling, one hand on her stomach and the other above her head. Her shirt did nothing to suppress the way her breasts jutted upward.

She furrowed her brow and turned to him. He couldn't ignore the punch of her stare, or how it diverted blood from his contented stomach. Flipping to his side had the effect of bringing him closer to her.

She rolled onto her side. They were face-to-face, inches away. "Can I tell you a secret?"

"Always." She could tell him anything. As long as she didn't give him the silent treatment for another ten years.

"I didn't even apply to law school."

"No fucking way. Did Joan lose her shit?"

"She doesn't know," she whispered. She worried her lower lip, her gaze growing serious. "Maybe at one time I actively wanted to be a lawyer, but when I got to school, I had nothing more than a passing interest in law. I didn't want to do it for a living. Except..." She pursed her lips.

"Another secret?"

"Hell, yeah. This is better than fireman gossip."

She giggled. "I got an animal science minor when I did my bachelor's. And I finished the major when I was in business school. Mom and Dad have never seen my transcripts. They just sent the money I needed."

"What did Oliver say?"

"I never told him."

The warm glow that ignited inside of him was instantaneous. She felt comfortable enough around him to reveal major details about her life that she couldn't admit to her mom and hadn't admitted to her fiancé.

"So in a perfect world"—not Moore, he knew without asking—"you'd be a rancher."

She nodded and lay her head on the bed, crossing her arms. The angle looked awkward, but she hadn't moved away. "In a world where I had land and money and lived in a town that's full of nothing but good memories. Now, I'm relegated to magazines and the Sunday farm and ranch morning show on TV."

"Are all the memories bad?" he asked softly.

"Truthfully? There are a lot of good ones, but my mind does this cool trick where it fixates on the teasing. On the comparisons to my brothers. And the feeling that I have nothing here to build a life with." It was like slow motion. She unfurled an arm and touched the side of his face. "But I have some memories that I return to. They involve a guy.

He used to sneak into my room, and I could tell him anything."

He caught her wrist and turned her arm. Gently, he pressed a kiss to the base of her palm.

"I've missed that guy—for so long."

"I missed you too." He caught her gaze. "That is, if I'm the guy."

Her lips curled. "Maybe it was you."

He growled and tugged her close. "Let me help you remember."

Sliding his arms around her, he rolled her to her back and spread himself over her. Their legs were twined together, and his body lit up like a Christmas tree. Desire surged though him and her happy sigh only encouraged him. Their clothing did nothing to dampen the effect on his body.

Dropping his head, he caught her mouth in a long, slow kiss. She tasted sweet, branding the flavor of pumpkin pie into him. It would forever be his favorite dessert.

Sweeping his tongue inside her mouth, he was met with her eager licks but he kept his pace slow, sensual. This wasn't the rushed first time of teenagers. He was a man holding the woman of his dreams in his arms. This no-frills motel was as good as the Ritz. The comforter might as well be goose down instead of a threadbare secondhand quilt.

She opened her legs and rocked into him. He fit her perfectly. The strength in her legs only made him think of how tightly she could clench around him when she was coming. And the way her breasts pressed against him—what would they be like unrestrained, waiting for his touch, begging for his mouth?

Tunneling his hands under her shirt, he lifted it up at the same time. She broke the kiss to help him, also rolling up his shirt until they had to break apart while she swept her top off and he did the same with his.

The material cupping her creamy flesh was teal, like her eyes, with a lacy overlay that let her nipples play peekaboo. Pulling down the bra, he sucked one peak into his mouth as he wound his arms around the back of her to undo the garment.

She sighed when her breasts popped free, and he tossed the bra off the side of the bed. His pants were tight, cutting into his erection, amplifying the throb. He was living out his dream. All those years ago, he'd convinced himself that he wanted one more chance, and he thought he'd walked away from it that night in the bathroom.

His chance was now, and he'd been lying to himself. One time, a million times, it wouldn't be enough with her. It would be impossible to get enough of her. And it wasn't because their time together was limited. He was going into this with his eyes wide open. She planned to move. He planned to stay. But they were together for now after being apart for so long.

She arched her back into him, murmuring his name. The flush he loved was back in her cheeks and his ego preened at being the one to put it there. Her lips were parted, and her hair was mussed as she gazed at him. Keeping the contact, he kissed his way down the satin skin of her stomach. She squirmed as if hit with a sudden pang of self-consciousness, but he was determined to cure her of that.

"You're beautiful, Bridge." He flicked the button free on her pants and slowly ran the zipper down. "I want to see all of you."

Her gaze flicked to the lamp with its thick shade and its weak attempt to light the room. Her throat worked like she had to think about it.

"Would you be more comfortable if I was naked too?" Rearing up on his knees, he undid his jeans and stripped them off, underwear at the same time. Next came his socks, because as comfortable as he was in his own skin, wearing nothing but a pair of socks wasn't the epitome of sexy.

She sucked in a quiet breath. "That's not making me feel better, Caleb."

"I'm just a normal guy."

Her gaze dipped to his straining erection. He'd never been harder in his life, and her gaze was like a roaring fire licking over dry logs. "There's nothing normal about you." She feigned a curious look. "Do you work out?"

He chuckled and hooked his fingers over the waist of her pants and tugged. "Sometimes."

She propped herself on her elbows as he worked her bottoms down. He stopped partway, when she was bared to him. Her legs still trapped in the material, he planted a kiss on her exposed flesh and inhaled the sweet, musky scent of her desire.

"I don't know if I'm going to last. Just looking at you makes me feel like I have no control over my body. These curves you're self-conscious about are the most beautiful things I've ever seen. And I'd think that if you ate twelve more pies. A day. For years. And your height. My God, Brigit. Those legs? I can't get enough of you. I think *you're* beautiful."

"I—" Her mouth worked, but no other words came out. Shattering vulnerability cascaded through her features before they settled again.

She wiggled out of her pants and pulled him over her, her hands cupping his face. "No one's ever made me feel like you do."

He kissed her but couldn't continue until he addressed the only concern he had before taking this further. "I have a condom in my wallet, but it's been there so long it might not be the best quality." He'd never been the type to scrounge through town looking for sex, but he also never tried hard to be boyfriend material. The only regret he had about any of that was that not having a fresh condom might put a stop to this moment.

"I'm… I went to the doctor the day after the breakup. I felt so dirty that I wanted it all checked out." Her eyes flashed fire. "And I made sure to tell them why. But they didn't find anything wrong and I'm still on the pill."

"I never go without protection, but we'll use what we've got." He rolled away to grab his wallet off the end table. The condom was on in no time and he had no idea how his hands didn't shake.

When he was done, she tugged him back and brushed her thumb along his lower lip. She opened herself to him. He shifted his hips until his cock slid through her wetness, but he didn't push in right away.

This night was about taking his time. And being with Brigit was going to test his ability to last beyond a few pumps.

He pressed his lips first on one side of her mouth, then the other. Tasting her was becoming his new favorite activity. This time when he moved down her body, he teased her other nipple. She writhed under him, but he steadied her with a hand at her core. So wet. For him.

"Caleb." The need in her voice, the near whine—she was in as bad a state as him. Good.

"I'll take care of you." He kneeled between her knees and skimmed his hands up her inner thighs, pressing them farther apart.

The dim light of the room cast shadows across her damp, glistening curls. He planned to squeeze every second out of this moment as he lowered his head and licked through her slit to her clit. Her moan filled the room and she arched her back. He held her to him and licked and sucked, changed tempo, altering his rhythm. Just as she was about to crest, her body tight, her knees drawing up, he backed off.

"You're a tease," she gasped.

The second time he brought her close to the brink, he backed off the pressure and slid a finger inside. Liquid heat gripped him, and she moved. He let her set the pace, just along for the ride.

She twisted her hands in his hair as she rode his palm. Heat flooded from her as she threw her head back and cried out.

He didn't move as she shuddered in bliss—he was committing the whole experience to memory. Some people called Brigit the Ice Queen. In high school, they'd joked that she couldn't be homecoming queen because she'd already built her own ice palace to reside over. But Brigit was anything but frigid. And she trusted him to see this side of her. It was humbling.

He understood this woman, just like she seemed to understand his need to be wanted by one person over all others. Since he'd lost his grandparents, he'd been adrift. He had friends. His coworkers were a makeshift family he saw a few times a week. He trusted them with his life, and they did the same with him.

This was different. Brigit didn't have to be here. She wanted to be here. With him. They weren't just hanging out as friends. She'd given herself to him.

Crawling up her delectable body, he couldn't quit touching her, with his hands, his mouth, his body.

"That was the most amazing thing I've ever seen," he confessed.

"That was…the most amazing thing to experience." She tilted her head, her hair fanning out behind her. She was his angel, if only for tonight.

Lust pounded through him. It was like his body could

only be so giving and generous before he turned into a selfish hedonist. He needed relief, but the desperation was only because this was Brigit. None of his past experiences, not even those with her, factored into tonight. He couldn't remember them if he tried, but he did know that he'd never had such tenuous control over himself. He held himself at her opening, rocking his hips to wet the tip of his cock. Nothing but pleasure for her.

She cradled him, wrapping her legs around him. He thrust inside, the air squeezing out of his lungs as pleasure blazed over his shaft, coalescing at the base of his spine. Good God, he wasn't going to last long.

She adjusted to his size, each wiggle of her hips sending him closer to the edge. Her little smile wrenched his heart. "No, nothing normal about you."

A long, tortuous groan escaped him. He tried to keep from thrusting like a fool. "This is... I... Next time, I'll last. I promise."

He started pumping. She met him with equal force, their skin slapping together, moans and grunts echoing through the room. His whole body tightened, and he threw his head back. One more push, two, and he was jerking his release inside of her, every quiver and clench of her body extending his rapture.

Eventually, his shudders subsided, and he collapsed into the warm cocoon of her body.

She ran her hands over his back, into his hair, and peppered her lips along his face.

This moment. It wasn't his home or hers, the room itself was a stale sauna, and he doubted his best friend would thank him for causing a rift between Brigit and her parents. Yet somehow, this moment was perfect. Only one question overshadowed his bliss. What could he do to make sure she didn't walk away from him—again?

CHAPTER 10

Water pounded down on Brigit in the shower, but she hardly noticed. She was pushed up against the wall of the shower, Caleb was inside of her, and she was so close to coming she had no idea how many times she'd shouted yes.

Waking up next to Caleb made the best morning ever, and sex in the shower was the red-hot cherry on top. This man made her feel dainty, almost fragile, as his strong body thrust into hers. She was anchored to him with her legs wrapped around his waist, but his hands dug into her as he held on. If he went down, she'd go with him, but to be honest, there wasn't enough room in the stall to even sit.

He widened his stance and funneled more power into his thrusts. She was done. Her orgasm hit and the way her voice ricocheted off every surface in the bathroom, anyone outside would know she was done too.

Caleb grunted her name and joined her with his own climax.

This was their third time together since she'd arrived. He'd made a condom run sometime in the middle of the night, then once he'd climbed between the sheets, they'd been all over each other.

He slipped out of her but held her close, and not because there was no other way to stand together without touching in the small space. Gingerly, she lowered her legs with Caleb's help. His sexy smile went straight to her heart. His hair was plastered over his forehead, giving him that edgy look she'd always associated with him.

He gave her a long, lazy kiss before leaving her to finish cleaning up. A few minutes later, she stepped out to a towel waiting for her on the sink—closer to her than the hook on the wall.

This night had been like a mini vacation. Stress had sluiced off her and she'd let herself enjoy being with Caleb. They'd talked about his ranch, his fears of keeping it profitable, and how worried he was the house wouldn't come to fruition. She'd asked him more about his childhood. The way he could openly discuss the hazards of living with his grandparents while technically being in the custody of his mom was humbling. She hadn't known what his youth was like, only that he'd accepted his lot and rolled with it. Because there was nothing else he could have done.

She'd had a safe and stable home and responsible parents. Her brothers might have been pains in the butt growing up, but they'd all gotten along. As adults, they'd grown apart, even her and Justin, but they were there if she ever needed them.

Caleb's grandparents had left him with so much, but they were still gone. He'd made his way through life with very little support. She'd had all the support in the world and still did really, but she lacked what Caleb had made for himself. A place to call her own. She still had to find her own place in so many ways.

By the time she left the bathroom, holding the towel in

front of herself, Caleb was already dressed. He'd stacked her clothing neatly on the bed and was perched next to it, his elbows propped on his knees and his chin in his hands.

"Are you here for the whole weekend?" she asked, her gaze dropping to her clothing. Dressing in front of Caleb seemed so intimate. It went a level beyond what they'd experienced together so far. Though she'd had long-term relationships—that maybe someday she'd quit regretting—she'd been in this place before, getting ready to walk out after a night of simple fun. But then, it had been different... She had done her makeup before leaving the bathroom.

Yet since coming home, she doubted she could find her mascara, most of her wardrobe no longer fit, and now her hair hung damp over her shoulders. Had Caleb ever been this close to someone?

Did he have any regrets about how he'd acted?

No, he had no reason to be.

"I work tomorrow morning," Caleb answered. "So only one more night in Chez Moore-tel. But it's really not bad, as long as we leave a window cracked and you're here."

Her heart warmed so much she almost forgot she was soggy and naked. Almost.

He looked from her to her clothing. "Are you shy? After what we've done?" His lopsided grin wasn't just incredulous. There was a hint of hurt.

"I just feel so exposed."

He cocked a brow and his dark gaze swept her body. "I exposed you all night long."

"But you're dressed." She clutched the towel tighter and spilled what she'd been thinking. "I've never been like this. I always made sure I was..." Stupid. She couldn't come out and say it. Would it be insulting to him to mention her past, one she could've had with him? "Presentable."

"How?"

She couldn't get frustrated with him. The guy rolled out of bed ready to go. "I put my face on." The rest poured out of her like a fence had been knocked down and the cows had found greener pasture. "And do more than finger-comb my hair. I always wear the good underwear, which usually means uncomfortable. And I'm not so…corn-fed." She huffed out a breath. "I've been hungry for years." Had she really admitted all that?

"Sounds exhausting."

"It is." It sounded pathetic too.

"Well." Caleb settled back on his elbows and crossed one leg over his knee. "It's up to you. I'll give you privacy, or you can dress while I watch everything and get uncomfortably hard."

Her pulse jumped. She liked the idea of him watching too much. "Think you can get hard again so soon?"

"Watching you? Yes." Complete confidence. "I'm already halfway there."

A flush crept up her body. She had to know if she really had that affect on him. She dropped the towel and grabbed her underwear first. It wasn't plain white, but it was pretty close. These were one of the oldest pairs she owned. One of the pairs that she'd kept at the house in her old dresser, just in case.

Caleb tracked her like a hawk circling its prey.

Next was her bra. There was no enticing way to get a bra on, but she might change her opinion based on how Caleb adjusted himself.

She stepped into her jeans, her jiggling breasts and wiggling hips catching his attention.

He groaned. "This is the best thing I've ever seen."

She nearly rolled her eyes but couldn't stop her grin. "It'll be my turn for a show next time."

"Next time?"

She stopped, her shirt hanging from her hands. "Yes?"

He sat forward and pulled her between his knees. "So what is this? Us?"

"I think…" What did she think? She was torn in two. There was the girl who loved her home and hadn't regretted a moment with Caleb. There was also the woman who'd worked hard for her education and wanted to use it. She wanted to carve out her own niche in the world. "I think we're still going in different directions in life, but as long as we're traveling together for a while, there's no reason we can't be together. If…you want to?"

"I've wanted you my whole life, Brigit. I'll take what I can get."

Her phone buzzed and they both froze.

"This is ridiculous." She reached for it in the nightstand. Huh, she wasn't so self-conscious about being shirtless around Caleb. She chuckled when she read the message from Justin out loud. "'Are you bringing my main mode of escape back? I'm one more sigh away from riding horse to the hardware store.'"

"I'd better let you go rescue him." He pressed his lips against her stomach.

She tossed the phone on the bed and hugged him to her. She had a day full of nothing ahead of her. More job searching. Trying not to act awkward around her parents. Begging Justin to do some of the chores to escape any tension.

Sounded awesome. "What are your plans for the day?"

He let her go. "You made such a good case about switching minerals and supplements to decrease my open rate, I thought I'd wander through town and see what there is."

He could call her beautiful again and it wouldn't make her glow so much. He was taking her advice to switch minerals and see if that helped improve his calving numbers.

"What if I caught a ride to town with Justin and met up with you?" She shrugged into her shirt to cover a sudden case of nerves. It was like she'd asked him out. She'd never asked a guy out.

"Seriously? I'd love having your expertise at my disposal."

"It's only book knowledge, so…"

"So it's more than I have. And it might be more than the person on shift at the farm supply store has." He handed her the keys. "I would've started the pickup but since it's the only set of keys, I figured today would be the one day a car thief drives by."

"After the sauna in here, a cold truck sounds nice."

"I'll warm you up later."

She grinned. "Deal."

He walked her out and she pulled away first. When Mom had busted them together as teenagers, Mom had hauled her away like a felon off to prison. Brigit had glimpsed Caleb in the rearview mirror, his head hanging low, his hands shoved in the pants he'd hastily put back on.

She glanced at Caleb in the mirror. Caleb waved before he swung his lithe form into his truck. Heat blasted across her body. What a man. And she was seeing him again. She bit her bottom lip and sighed.

How times changed.

If I sit here any longer, they're going to call the cops on me.

Caleb glanced around the half-full parking lot. The major Black Friday run was over, and he'd been buried deep inside Brigit's willing body for most of it.

Best Black Friday ever.

But she hadn't shown yet. She'd surprised him and messaged him to ask where he'd be and when. Without her own vehicle, she was dependent on Justin. And if Justin up and left her, she'd have to ask her mom. An image flashed through his mind of prim Joan Walker sneaking out of the house to puncture a tire or remove the battery cables so she could blame a vehicle breakdown for not being able to deliver her precious daughter into his dirty arms.

A silly worry, but one that felt more likely with each minute that ticked by.

He needed to talk to Justin. The man's sister had been in Caleb's bed all night. Justin had loaned his vehicle to Brigit, but he probably hadn't expected her to spend the night. What did he think?

A loud rumble punctured his doubt spiral. Justin swung his pickup into the spot next to Caleb's. Justin lifted his chin and turned to say something to Brigit as she climbed out.

Caleb got out. He might as well find out if there was bad blood between them. Brigit slanted him a small smile as she walked around to the passenger side. She didn't stop but got inside like she knew he had to clear the air with Justin.

Justin lowered the window. "What's up?"

"Just wanted to know… We good?"

Justin's gaze slid to where Brigit was settling in, then back. "Because you kept Brigit out past her curfew?"

"Well…"

"Kidding, man." Justin grinned, but turned serious. "Not that you or Brigit need my approval, but if I'd ever thought you were bad for her, you wouldn't have been to my house so often."

Caleb nodded, a lump forming in his throat. Justin's support was no little deal, and he hadn't realized how much the secret had bothered him until its weight was lifted from his chest. "I guess I need to get right by your parents, but I don't know if she's ready for that level of commitment."

"Dad just wants Brigit to be happy and he's always gotten

along with you. Mom might be a little raw that you're stealing her time with her baby girl, but I don't think you need to be terrified of her like you have been since I've known you."

Caleb cast him a droll look.

Justin shrugged. "Okay, I mean, I don't think it's as personal as you think. Brigit was kind of a loner as a kid and we all worried about her."

"She still plans on leaving."

"Can you blame her?" Justin draped an arm over the steering wheel and peered out the window. "It was kind of like, 'Hey, all the land and cattle you worked growing up, we're giving Travis everything. Fly, little birdie.' We had the world open to us, but I don't know that either of us really wanted to go. I thought I did, but city life didn't agree with me. I got to come home because the guys expanded and needed extra help. But they're having kids and if they took on extra people, it'd be as a hired hand. I can't blame her for wanting more than to be someone's bitch her whole life."

"I don't, either," Caleb said quietly.

Justin looked directly at him. "I know. And that's why I'm worried about you. Don't think I haven't noticed that you only had eyes for her when we were younger, and you've never been serious with anyone else. Now she's back and you're standing here asking for my blessing even when you know it's temporary."

Someone's bitch. Would that be how everyone saw it if by some miracle she stayed in Moore and built a life with him? Would that be how she felt?

Acid turned his breakfast sour. He'd be ecstatic, living the life he wanted with the woman he'd loved his whole life, while she'd be settling, doing the work he couldn't get to while he was on duty.

"I wish there were more job opportunities here."

"If there were, we'd have a population that hit five figures. Anyway." He flipped his truck into gear. "Let me know if she needs a ride home. I'm going out with Maisy tonight, but we can swing by and get her."

"I'd rather get chewed out by your mom than put Brigit through facing Maisy again."

Justin shifted back into park. "She said something similar. Were there really problems with Maisy?"

Other than the girl being selfish, arrogant, and callous and not one bit better as a woman? "I don't know specifics. I just know there were."

A muscle jumped in Justin's jaw. "I guess this might be the last date, then."

"Let's hope it goes better than when you two broke up junior year."

Justin frowned as he tried to remember. "What, you mean my car getting keyed? That wasn't her."

The hell it wasn't. "She just didn't get caught. But it wasn't a coincidence that it happened while you were at your rebound's house."

His brow furrowed. "I just can't picture Maisy doing that."

"She's obsessed with you. Be careful." Caleb tapped on the truck door and turned to his own.

Brigit was scrolling through her phone.

He opened the door. "Should we go through here first?"

"Sure." Brigit hopped back out. "I have a specific brand in mind."

No one gave them more than a second glance as they wandered through the store. He was in here enough and Brigit had been coming since she was a kid.

"While I'm in town, I should look at a new kind of colostrum replacer." She pulled out her phone. "Justin said he just bought what they had on hand, but he's had to use it more than he thought for multiples. He asked me to look into the best brand."

"It's probably the same department. I doubt they have much for sheep around here." They both angled toward the back of the store where the displays for minerals and supplements were.

A man in a red frock turned the corner. Teddy. Caleb put a lot of his orders through the guy. "Can I help you with— Oh, Caleb. What can I do for you?"

"I'm thinking of changing up my mineral based on what she recommends."

Teddy glanced at Brigit and right back to him. "Is there something wrong with what you're using?"

Brigit rattled off the brand she'd mentioned earlier. "I think it's better suited for this area."

Teddy only spared her another brief look before turning back to Caleb. "The mineral you order through us is just fine. They're all the same, really. Fourteen minerals."

"They're not all the same," Brigit said tightly. "Do you carry it or not?"

Teddy eyed the bags piled on the pallets, each with their own labels claiming they were the best in the market. "We've never seen the need to. The ranchers in this area haven't mentioned the name." Extra stress on *ranchers in the area*. "But we have some fliers if you decide you need a change." Teddy turned and plucked fliers from the front of each brand.

Caleb snuck a peek at Brigit. Her pinched features held back a maelstrom of emotion. Her ice mask had slid into place.

Teddy handed the papers to Caleb.

Brigit's lips thinned. "Where's your sheep colostrum?"

Teddy blinked. "Oh, uh, it's around the corner. But Caleb raises cattle."

Caleb chortled. "She's well aware I raise cattle, Teddy."

Brigit lifted a cool brow and stared Teddy down. "Sheep colostrum."

"Oh yes. Yes, sorry." Teddy rounded the endcap of the aisle. "Again, we don't have much variety, but any of these will work for the occasional 4H project."

"It's not a 4H project," she said tightly. "My brother's a sheep rancher."

"Oh, Justin Walker?" Teddy craned his neck around. "Is he here?"

"No." She didn't elaborate but stepped in front of Teddy to study the labels on the colostrum.

"O-Okay. Let Justin know he can talk to me anytime."

Caleb didn't have to see Brigit's face to know she was rolling her eyes so hard her irises disappeared. But again, no drama.

Teddy left them, and Caleb leaned over to whisper, "How pissed are you?"

"I'll have to have you or Justin talk to Teddy to find out for me." She pivoted. "They could use some education on the products available out there."

"Or you could give them a talking-to. Make them listen."

She didn't react. Did she think he wasn't serious? "Let's go to the vet clinic. Bunny's clinic offers some of the specialty brands this store refuses to carry. If she has what I'm looking for, you'll have to special order it through them, but you don't pay shipping."

"Your cousin sells mineral at the vet clinic?"

"You can order it through them. I think once my dear friend Teddy realizes what a good product it is, and what a good fit it'll be, he'll start carrying it. Bunny doesn't want to compete with them, but you know how hard it is for old-time ranchers to change their ways."

He did. The Walkers had some of the best expertise in the

area, but since they weren't at the bar like they used to be, he didn't have a chance to talk to them as often. Only since Justin's return had he been able to get updated advice on supplements, decreasing open rates, and the overall longevity of his cows. A healthy cow was a calving cow.

"Vet clinic it is." As they walked out of the store, another question popped into his head. Teddy might not take her seriously, but he did. "You know anything about using sorghum for silage instead of corn?"

She gave him a sidelong look. "Have you asked Teddy?" Her lips twitched. Good. Teddy might not have known what a gold mine of information Brigit was, but Caleb did. "The answer is yes. I wrote a paper on it in college. My professor even asked for my references for a review he was writing for an ag journal."

As he drove across town, Brigit covered the pros and cons of switching the way he fed his cows during the winter months when grass wasn't available. He'd heard a few comments here and there about the type of silage making a difference but to have Brigit cover the topic so thoroughly? A guy couldn't Google that shit and not get lost for hours in conflicting information.

It was often how he spent the evenings of his shifts at the fire department.

He put an order in through the clinic, and once they were done, he took her out to eat.

"I didn't think the Brown House Café would be this busy today." Brigit looked around at the booths filled with diners. The tapping of silverware on glass plates made a background chorus that drowned out the twangy old country music playing from the speakers.

Caleb liked the food here, but he'd smell like grease and coffee all day. "I don't recognize anyone."

Brigit's gaze turned solemn as she studied him. "I'm not

afraid of being seen out with you. I've just had enough of others in my business, and I know what people will assume when they see us together."

"We are together. For now."

Her mouth twisted in a half frown. "I feel like the bad guy."

He reached across the table and grabbed her hand. "I didn't mean to sound like a dick. It was mostly a reminder for myself."

She gave his hand a squeeze and went back to her menu. "What are we going to do after this? After dinner, I mean."

Subtle change of topic. One that was welcome given the nebulous terms of their not-quite relationship. "I'm going to run back out to the ranch before I turn in for the night. I can give you a ride home when I do. I'm sure your mom would like some time with you before she heads back."

"Right." She lifted her gaze above the menu. "Maybe we can make a pit stop before that? Maybe back to your room?"

A swirl of awareness gathered, a small funnel of anticipation. After lunch, Brigit would be his dessert. "Whatever the lady wants."

CHAPTER 11

$\mathcal{B}$rigit tightened the wire stretcher along the portion of fence line getting sealed together. Her breath puffed in front of her like she'd taken a long drag off a cigar. The wind whipped at her coat and hood, the fabric crackling like paper from the frigid temps. So much different than waking up in Caleb's warm embrace this morning. It was their third night together since he'd returned to the house Sunday.

Mom had asked if she was going to spend more time with Caleb, and Brigit had said that he was working Saturday and she'd see him later. She also slipped in that Caleb hadn't wanted to interfere with their time together. The rest of which had been spent pretending Thursday and Friday had never happened.

After the long weekend, she and Caleb had started sleeping in the same bedroom. Justin acted like it was business as usual and didn't comment on the new sleeping arrangement.

Justin crouched next to her. The section of fence they

were repairing was almost done. "I'm glad we found this before the snow starts flying."

"You don't want to tromp through a foot of snow to chase down sheep?"

Justin grunted. "I hope it's only a foot."

"We've almost made it to December without snow."

"Snow this time of year is better than in the spring, when lambs are coming."

He finished attaching the new piece of wire and she took off the wire stretcher.

He piled the tools in his arms and stood. "You might want to get to Minneapolis sooner than later."

Yeah. That. She rose and turned her back to the wind. "I know. Brock said he'd lend me a car and Josie would take care of the insurance."

"Did you tell Caleb?" Justin asked. "Maybe he'll go with you."

"He works Friday." But she'd thought of that, taking her cowboy to the city, watching him cause whiplash in city girls everywhere he went.

Justin cocked a light brow. "You're on a knowing-his-schedule basis?"

"Shut up." She opened the backdoor of his truck so he could set the tools inside.

"Seriously though. The weather might set in earlier than predicted. Think it'd be held against you if you got snowed in?"

She almost shrugged it off, but no, this job interview was important to her. It was for a good position. The manager she'd talked to was excited about her education.

We don't get many loan officers with not only an ag background, but an actual degree in both business and ag.

The credit union that had called her was renowned for

their work with farmers and ranchers, especially the big dairy farms dotting the Minnesota landscape.

She was perfect for the job. Not only that, they had several branches, which offered her plenty of upward mobility. She'd only live hours from Moore, as well as being an easy flight away from her parents, and she'd get to live in the city, where she could be blessedly anonymous.

"Think I should leave tonight? It'd be another night for the hotel."

"My portion of the ranch will cover it."

"Justin, you're already feeding me and putting me up." She was on the short route to thirty, but she was a charity case to her own family.

"Consider it payback for opening my eyes to the crazy that is Maisy."

He'd been in a foul mood all weekend. She should've recognized it. Once upon a time, Maisy had caused the same swings in her. "She showed her true colors?"

He blew out a hard breath. "I asked her if she ever teased you while we were growing up. She denied it, but I said my twin wasn't a liar."

"And then she lost it?"

"No, still denied it. But I believe you and Caleb." Since when did Caleb know Maisy had taunted her relentlessly? "I tried another angle. I mean, Maisy's a good time, but I can't be with her if she wears a mask around me. So I said you and I were twins. And that you'd always come first."

"Oh God."

He nodded once. "And then she blew. Went nuclear."

"Hats off to you. I only know her cruel side. Her rage must've been blinding."

"She hit me."

Brigit gasped. "She did what?" All those missed opportunities to deck the girl and she'd walked away and let it fester inside.

"A slap, then that thing where she's pummeling me with both fists while I hold her away." His shoulders hunched. He rubbed his chest like he was bruised and it hurt.

"I'm sorry. You deserve better." She meant it. Her brother might be guarded or aloof or seem cool and uncaring—and wow, didn't that sound like herself? But at the end of the day, he was all about family.

Guess they were similar in that aspect.

"I'd like to think so, but the joke might end up on me."

"Because the other girl got engaged?"

"No." He looked up at the sky and for the first time in… ever…his calm fractured. His voice cracked as he said, "Maisy claims she's pregnant."

"Holy shit. She's lying, right? I mean you haven't been seeing her long."

He let out a sigh and dropped his head. "I hope so, but I've been searching online and shit and… She could be. If she is, is it mine? I dunno."

"What if… Shit, Justin." Yeah. Her brother would want to be a part of his kid's life. Hell, they all would. But Maisy would wield that kind of power with ruthless cruelty.

"I just… There's nothing to do until one, I know she's pregnant. And two, if it's mine." His face twisted with unseen pain. "But if she was okay pummeling me, how can I leave a baby to her mercy? I've heard Caleb's stories."

Ice crystallized in her veins. She'd only just started hearing Caleb's stories about life with Adele.

She put her hands on his shoulders. "First, we find out if she's pregnant. Then we go from there and you'll have half the county on your side."

He nodded, but she'd never seen him so defeated. But he had all the support in the world. And it reminded her that

Caleb had no one. She was leaving tonight to interview for a job that would take her away from him, and from Justin, and from all the family that was helping her out. Leaving for an interview didn't feel right. Not when it was a precursor to leaving for good.

Maybe she would call Caleb and see if there was any way he could go with her.

IT WAS weird to not drive the entire way, but Caleb was happy to be a passenger. Riding in a car instead of a truck was odd as well, but with Brigit driving, he'd hop in anything. She parked under the canopy of the hotel.

"I can go check in. Wait here." Brigit slipped out, the sparkles on the butt of her jeans flashing under the hotel's lights. She disappeared inside.

When it had been his turn to drive, she'd researched hotels while chattering with him, probably to keep herself awake. That part of his job was ingrained in him. If he was awake at night, he was up. Only when his head hit the pillow did he relax.

When he'd told her that he could go with her but had to be home by Sunday, she'd been delighted. He'd barely managed to switch shifts, but once the guys heard he wanted to go out of town with a woman—and not just any woman, but Brigit Walker—they'd helped arrange the schedule despite his pleas that it wasn't serious.

He could lie to them about it, but he couldn't fool his heart. This felt serious. Waking up to her every morning this week had felt serious. Justin knowing that Caleb was sleeping with his sister rang with all kinds of serious.

Caleb stared up at the hotel. How different would his job be in the big city? He had plenty of experience, he had the respect of his boss, but fighting house fires and grass fires and the occasional business's false alarm was a little different than a building where the number of floors hit double digits. Even the false alarms in this place would make his head spin.

It'd be cool to talk shop with some firefighters here. Was the job market competitive, would he have an edge up because of his experience, or would they laugh him out of the city?

What was he thinking? He still had his grandparents' ranch. *His* ranch. He had eighty creatures that relied on him to do his job so they didn't suffer. Being a rancher and a fireman meant he was more a part of the big world than the kid who'd been shut in a closet for the night so his mom could party. He meant something to the food supply of the nation. He meant something to the safety of the town he lived in.

When he was a kid, people looked past him. Or they saw him and immediately looked away. Now, when he walked through town, he nodded to folks all around him, exchanging hellos. They either knew him as a fellow rancher —and a respected one—or they knew him from his work in the community. Places where he helped inspect fire alarm systems knew him by name, and parents recognized him from the awareness carnivals his crew did for kids. Local students passed him in the grocery store, saying, "Hey, I know you."

His adult life was so different than when he'd been a kid, and yet it was the same town.

The anonymity Brigit craved in the city wouldn't suit him. He'd worked hard to be known for who he was, and he'd surpassed that to become respected. A big leap for a kid with a mom the town thought was a good-for-nothing partier.

Brigit trotted out the door, snagging his attention, a piece of paper and a set of card keys in her hand.

She opened the car door on a swirl of cold air. "We're on the seventh floor."

There wasn't a building in Moore with more than three levels. For work, he'd had to train with grain bins.

She parked, and they found their room. This place was nothing like the Moore-tel. The faint smell of chlorine floated on the air underneath the chemical-laden floral scent. His gaze strayed to the smoke alarms and the sprinkler heads. Seventh floor. He might have the ear gauges and a different hairstyle than the rest of his crew, but he was more of a country boy than he'd thought.

Brigit opened the door to their room. He didn't miss her soft inhale.

"Look at that." She went straight for the window. The curtains were open. The sun set early this time of year, but the lights of the city spread across the horizon. "It's gorgeous."

Caleb stood next to her. The view did have its own appeal. He preferred his front porch, back when he'd had a front porch. More like, he preferred the view from the end of his driveway after he'd cleared the trees around his place, before he turned onto the road, when the fields stretched out before him and the sky was like a dome over his own personal paradise.

"It's nice" was all he said.

Brigit glanced at him, but he couldn't decipher her expression. "We should close the curtains. I doubt anyone can see, but I'd rather err on the side of privacy."

"I don't think we'll wake up to any sheep eating the flower beds here."

She laughed. "It'd be a shock if we did." She flopped on the bed and stretched out. "That drive is too short for long stops but long enough to be uncomfortable."

He sat next to her. "What are we doing tomorrow?"

"Justin paid me for my work." She sighed, but Caleb thought reimbursement was justified. When Brigit wasn't applying for jobs, she was working around Justin's place or hopping in with Caleb to do chores. "I need a new outfit. I brought one that could work, but if I can get one that screams professional woman a little better, I'd like that."

"Shopping it is."

She popped her head up. "And they have outlet malls close by."

"Which are?"

Her forehead crinkled. "Brand-name stores for a discount."

"Ah." No wonder he'd never heard of them. If he couldn't find what he needed in town, he ordered it. He glanced down at himself. Same old black cowboy boots, his nicer pair of blue jeans, and a Moore Fire Department T-shirt with *Cruise* in block letters across the back. The clothing in his suitcase wasn't much different.

But it wasn't like he could do anything. Buying a new wardrobe wasn't in his budget. There'd be meals out, and he wasn't letting Brigit shoulder the whole trip. He saw the guilt reflected in her gaze each time she mentioned Justin paying her. She might want to make her own way in the world, but she enjoyed working with her family and hated taking money that could go back into the farm and ranch. Or into the accounts of her cousins who had kids to raise.

She flopped back. "But we don't have to worry about that until tomorrow. I don't think they're supposed to get as much snow here as home."

"Sounds like only an inch or two."

"So we're ready to turn in, then?" Her sultry question pushed aside all thoughts of money and job interviews. He had Brigit to himself and he was going to make the best of it.

CHAPTER 12

*B*rigit swirled around outside of the dressing room. "Does this say professional woman who desperately needs a job?" She'd found a black knit sweater dress on clearance, thick gray leggings in the discount bin, and a collared white plaid shirt for underneath the sweater—also on sale. All she needed was a thick belt and neck wrap and her ensemble would be complete.

She bit back a smile at Caleb's expression. He was perched in one of the two wingback chairs in the waiting area outside the changing rooms. Heat simmered in his eyes as his gaze stroked her legs. The charcoal gray knee-high boots were hers. A splurge from years ago, when she'd fit into the rest of her working-girl clothes.

A couple of women circled a rack of designer shirts, spying on Caleb out of the corners of their eyes. Brigit knew the feeling. He wasn't wearing a hat of any sort today. His hair was slicked back, his shaved sides bare, and his small ear gauges in. The way he was sitting only made his shoulders broader, and he'd kept to a soft black T-shirt, claiming his other shirts screamed country boy. Like that was a bad thing.

His dark blue jeans were a newer pair and exaggerated his swagger when he walked.

He was so hot.

"It says a lot of things not appropriate for me to say," he drawled. "Damn."

"I think it'll work too." She zoomed back into the changing room and changed back into the only outfit that had looked decent on her since she'd moved back home. It was one of the few things she had left that didn't fall into the realm of pajamas or chore wear. She tied off the sage-green wraparound cardigan over her cream long-sleeved shirt and black leggings. This outfit would've been fine, but a new one was a confidence booster.

And she needed one, being back in the city she'd lived in for so many years.

She stepped out. Caleb was paging through a women's magazine. He tossed it back on the table and unfolded his body. As he put on his coat, he twisted, his shirt tightening in all the right places. Her insides somersaulted. Why was he getting more potent the more she was around him? She'd never get over him. That was probably why the phone call offering the interview hadn't made her dance through the house. This link between them was only strengthening.

Checking out, she mused over the differences between Minneapolis and Moore. The clerk was polite and asked if she'd found everything okay. But there was no, "How's your mom and dad doing?" "I loved seeing your brother's sheep in the parade last summer." "Oh, that little nephew of yours is the spitting image of Travis."

She could probably go to the nearest farm supply and get taken seriously instead of someone like stick-in-the-mud Teddy ignoring her until she went away.

Those instances, she hated. All the times she'd gone to run errands with her dad and had been invisible—or worse, the times the guys had laughed at her interest. "Just like Daddy, isn't she?"

Friends didn't believe her when she recalled the time she'd actually heard, "Don't worry your pretty little head about power tools." That had been from a woman in her seventies.

Though Brigit did miss the personal touch. Like her fifth-grade teacher stopping her in the grocery store. "Oh, Brigit. Nice to see you back in town."

She'd been home long enough that people didn't ask her about school anymore. They seemed to accept that she was back, and they'd see her around again.

She was deep in thought as she slid into the driver's seat.

"Something wrong?" Caleb tapped his knees, watching her. Droplets from melted snow glistened in his hair. She wanted nothing more than to take him back to the hotel and cozy into the blankets. Maybe order some room service.

"Just thinking about how shopping here is different than home. Nothing serious."

"So where's this place you want to take me?"

She'd planned on taking him to a club she used to visit in college, after she turned twenty-one. But pumping bass was the last thing she wanted to deal with right now. Room service sounded better and better.

"The place I had in mind is actually a club and I'm not really in the mood for it."

"You mean I'm not dressed for it?"

Was he insecure about his appearance? "I think you could show up on the doorstep anywhere and get welcomed in. No, it's loud. I'm not up for loud."

"We could request a song with mooing in the background."

She chuckled. "Sheep are even quieter. I've been spoiled."

And she had been. Earlier, Justin had sent her a picture of

the yard covered in a blanket of snow. Pristine. Sparkling. Undisturbed. She was missing it to be here.

She shook the thought off. There'd be more snowfalls. "How 'bout a burger?"

"If I'm never up for a burger, you know something's wrong." He relaxed in his seat. "Surprise me."

The city wasn't quiet, but traffic was minimal as she wove through the streets, looking for a good place to eat, one that wasn't only about families but also not a noisy bar. She had some ideas, but she wanted something close to the hotel.

Caleb watched the city go by. Had he really never traveled? His mom had dragged him all over the county, but when she'd moved to another city, she'd left him behind.

A weight settled around Brigit's heart. She was nothing like his mother. She'd never shove a kid in a corner so she could party. But at the same time, she was planning to leave him behind as soon as she found something "better."

Her optimism for her job interview faded even more. This was a good thing. It was what she'd been working toward her whole life. She loved animals and ranching, but it wasn't a feasible career. She didn't have the capital to start her own business and it wasn't in her to swim against the tide of ingrained opinions and habits.

In the city, she didn't take things so personally.

But then, no one knew her enough for their slights to *be* personal.

She pulled into the next bar and grill that came up. A flashing cowboy boot on the sign clinched the deal.

"You didn't have to pick a place you thought I'd be comfortable in," Caleb said quietly.

She'd picked a place *she'd* be comfortable in. After she parked, she pointed to the letters underneath the sign. "I didn't want a bar that'd be too loud to talk in, but if it's gonna be loud it might as well be live music."

"You know the band?"

"Nope."

She clung to him on the slippery walk to the entrance. He opened the door and the chaos of voices and strumming guitars greeted them. A hostess in tight jeans and cowboy boots that had never seen green grass led them to a booth.

Caleb slid into the booth next to her, his arm slung around her back. They pored over the menu, hollering into each other's ears. This was exactly the noisy environment she'd wanted to avoid.

She decided on what to eat but kept staring at the menu. How was she going to live in the city now that she could picture Caleb here too? It had been easy to move here for college, not knowing a soul, and, more importantly, not having a history with anyone in it. But now?

Then there was Oliver. Until now, she'd ignored the irony of gravitating toward a guy from the hometown she'd been resolved to get away from. He hadn't gone to school in Minneapolis but had moved here for the job he'd eventually lost, which had prompted the move to Moore. And she'd glued herself to his side, all while ignoring the insulting way he treated her.

If she could, she'd go back and ignore the tidbit of information Mom had casually dropped. *Remember Oliver? He was a year ahead of you? I guess he sells insurance in Minneapolis now.* And she would definitely take back the casual stop into Oliver's workplace for an auto insurance quote.

Oliver was over. She might have to live in this city again if she got the job, but that didn't mean she'd return to her former lonely self, seeking a relationship in an attempt to feel complete.

Caleb leaned close. "Figure out what you want?"

She nodded and closed her menu, wishing she could do the same with her tumultuous thoughts. This bar was no different than any at home. Only she could relax better here. No one was looking at them and speculating about their future, how well they worked together, if she was too much woman for him, or whether or not she was good enough for him. If the residents of Moore knew she'd walked away from Caleb once already, being seen with him would send waves of gossip through town.

She could hear Maisy's nasal pitch stage-whispering to Priya even now. *He'd be much better off with someone like you. There's no way he could carry her over any threshold.*

What was it she'd said one time? *At least if you two ever sleep together, your clothes are big enough for him to borrow.*

Her musings were interrupted as they ordered. No sharing a burger or feeling guilty. No leaving hungry and salivating over the delicious smells emanating from the place. She was done with that. If she had to reconcile herself with a new bigger size, so be it.

In fact, she already had. Constant stomach pains were gone. Strength poured through her muscles when she worked the animals and fixed fence. And she slept better. She'd need a new wardrobe, but...fuck it.

Brigit scanned the bar. A few couples were on the dance floor, two-stepping through the cover of a popular country song.

This one used to be one of her favorites. But she'd quit listening to this style of music when she'd moved, sticking to clubs that played the latest hits—anything but country—and martini bars that couldn't spell Dierks Bentley, much less say his name.

When had she gotten so strict in shunning everything she'd grown up with? No wonder sneaking into animal science classes had been such a thrill.

Caleb noticed her gaze on the dance floor. "Wanna get a few steps in before they bring our food?"

The song ended, and they had a brief reprieve before they had to start yelling at each other again. "You dance?"

He smiled but it faded quickly. "Yeah. I discovered it was a good way not to, uh…go home alone."

"Oh." She patted his thigh. "I doubt you needed dancing for that."

"When I didn't have much at home, it helped to keep them running away in fear. No one wants to fall for the guy with no money."

"Then I guess you weren't bringing the right women home."

His solemn expression didn't change. "I knew I wasn't."

This man.

Another song started, the male lead crooning the first few lines a cappella. Caleb grabbed her hand and helped her out of the booth.

Dancing with him was…foreplay. His strong arms were around her, leading her left and right, maneuvering her where he wanted. She submitted to him, giggling when they bumped feet or when she tried to take over without knowing. His smile only widened as he spun her faster and held her closer.

His gaze strayed to where they'd been sitting. "We should go eat."

"Sure," she said with breathlessness that had nothing to do with the movement. Her body tingled from head to toe, her breasts were heavy, and she had an exquisite ache between her legs.

His gaze heated, promising all sorts of wicked things when they returned to the hotel room. "Then more dancing?"

"Absolutely."

～

THE ELEVATOR DOORS OPENED, and it was all Caleb could do not to tumble out. He hadn't had more than one drink, but he was tipsy with lust. Holding Brigit half the night, witnessing the way her fully clothed body moved and writhed, the smile on her face, and those moments when she bit her lower lip as she concentrated on the steps—they were intoxicating.

He secured her to his side and managed not to run to their room. His erection would've made that difficult anyway. His arm was around her shoulders with her shopping bags in the other hand. They moved in sync to the room door, both on the same page.

Dancing had always been a means to an end. A little two-step. A twirl here and there. It cut out the awkward chitchat and he could tell if his partner was receptive to more. But tonight...

He and Brigit had laughed, they'd slow-stepped like they were back at the middle school dance, and she'd let herself go. She'd trusted him enough to let herself go.

It was enough to take the sting out of keeping quiet while she passed all the trendy joints and settled on a bar and grill that could just as well be in Moore. Only they hadn't known anyone.

But he wasn't going to dig into her actions now. He just wanted her.

It took three swipes before their lock registered the key card. They stumbled in, the door slamming behind him. She let her coat slide to the floor and he did the same. Next, they each kicked their wet boots to the side.

Then he yanked her to him and planted his mouth on hers, too impatient to take the few steps to the bed. Fortunately, the outfit she'd tortured him in all night would be easy to get out of the way.

"I need you, now." He turned her around and her hands gripped the floor-length mirror.

She looked at her reflection and then at him. "Maybe we should…"

He crowded behind her and caught her gaze in the mirror. "No, we're not moving." Holding her attention, he yanked up her sweater and pulled down her leggings. He palmed the creamy flesh of her ass. "You can watch me fuck you." Proving at the same time that her height was perfect. She was perfect. That they fit perfectly.

Her lips parted, and she ground back into him. She probably didn't even realize the strength of her response. He didn't either. The mirror hadn't been planned, but he had a sudden need to make his mark, to take her in a way that she'd never forget.

Maybe in a way that she'd never be able to walk away from.

He'd always been a wishful thinker.

With one hand, he opened his pants and shoved all the material out of the way. With his other hand, he took care of protection. His shaft was hard and throbbing, and he stood so close to Brigit that her heat both soothed the ache and dumped fuel on the flame of his need.

Her sweater was bunched around her waist, but he left it. Feathering his hand around her hip, over the soft velvet of her skin, he dove his fingers between her folds. Her hot, wet flesh welcomed him, and she widened her stance to give him better access.

Licking along the rim of her ear, he circled her clit at the same time.

She moaned, but there was one problem.

"Open your eyes, Brigit."

Her eyelids fluttered open, the blue barely visible around her pupils. She was close, her body tight. But he wanted to be inside of her when she came.

Moving enough to slip himself between her legs, he

dragged his cock through her seam, coating himself. He did it again.

A low groan eked out of him. "Fuck, Brigit. I could come just like this."

She was rocking against his hand, her lip pinned between her teeth, her breath clouding the mirror. Gripping her hip with his free hand, he pulled her back, bending her slightly.

He kissed under her ear and held her as she shivered and ground into his hand. "Watch me."

She met his gaze. He pushed into her slowly, watching her expression change as he filled her. From pleasure to bliss. And when he moved, thrusting slowly, to ecstasy.

He barely moved, keeping his arm around her to stroke her clit.

"Caleb." A cloud of condensation gathered on the glass. She writhed against him, oblivious of her reflection, uncaring of what she revealed to him. The way her desire played across her face, flushing her cheeks, was the most erotic show he'd ever seen.

He only hoped to last long enough to climax with her. "Come with me, Bridge."

A whine came from her and she tightened around him, going so molten he was shoving over his peak and growling her name as his body went rigid.

"Caleb!" She clenched his shaft so tightly he could barely move. It was too much. Too much sensation. Too much emotion. Too much—but never enough.

He loved how she said his name when she came. He loved when they orgasmed together. He loved her—he had forever.

She trembled in his arms as he buried his head in her nape and tried to catch his breath and keep them both up.

When she quieted, he withdrew and kicked his pants off the rest of the way. He squatted and helped her out of her leggings, then rose and stripped her top off. Sweeping her into his arms, he carried her to the bed, setting her feet down only so he could whip the covers back. She dragged him in with her.

He circled his arms around her and covered them up. "I need a few minutes, then I have more planned."

"Mm. I do have to sleep too." She yawned and snuggled closer. "And pack so we can leave right after the interview."

She wanted to leave after the interview? Her interview was at eleven. It'd take an hour, tops.

"No more plans for the city after your interview?" he asked.

"Not really. I shouldn't spend any more money I might need for moving, and I don't want to risk you being late for work. There's more snow coming. We can't afford to be stranded."

It sounded logical. Her words made sense. But the disappointment cascading through him was anything but. First the bar and grill, and now she didn't want to spend any more time with him in the big city. This was their first opportunity to travel together, get away from everything, and have some time to themselves.

For him, it'd been a time to ponder his life. Where was he going? Or rather, where could he go? He loved his ranch. It meant the world to him. But if keeping it meant he'd live a long life alone, it wasn't exactly serving the purpose Grandma and Grandpa had bought it for. They'd worked the land so they could build a family, and while it hadn't been the brood of kids they'd hoped for, they'd raised Mom and him.

But Brigit wanted to go home. Was it because that was where she thought he belonged? They wouldn't be here for her big interview if Moore was where she thought *she* belonged.

ave you heard yet?

Brigit typed in her reply. *No.*

She didn't write, *I told you I'd tell you when I heard.* Every day for the last two weeks, Mom had been sending the same question like it was a compulsion. Mom was just a little excited. *Such a good position. Oh, you'd be perfect for it. I can just picture it.*

And there it was. Mom's unfailing confidence in her ability. Mom's unshakable faith. She was the reason Brigit worked so hard.

But it'd been a month since the trip to Minneapolis. The person she'd interviewed with said they had several applicants and some were flying in from out of state, one was even international, and they weren't going to offer the job to anyone before Christmas—which had been last week. No other places had called offering her an interview, but her inbox had filled with a few variations of *Thank you for your interest in this position. We're sorry to say...* She'd applied to five more jobs, and with more reluctance than she cared to admit, she'd widened her search to other cities as well.

"Ready already?" Caleb sauntered into the room after his shower, a towel slung low over his hips.

She was dressed, but she wasn't ready. Justin had asked them to go with him to the bar for New Year's Eve. He probably wanted them as a buffer to the insanity Maisy had infused into his life. She was pregnant—the positive test had been shipped express to the house. Brigit had signed for the package.

Then there were the phone calls. And messages. And pages of texts. Justin had been imprisoned on the ranch for the last month and he wanted to go out. Brigit and Caleb had decided to make that happen.

She had no desire to get caught in the crossfire, but this wasn't about her. It was about her twin and he'd done so much for her. Besides, she couldn't escape the feeling that somehow she'd disappointed Caleb in Minneapolis. He hadn't said anything—and she'd asked. He wasn't acting differently, but there was a heaviness in the air between them. A separation, even though they were closer than ever.

"I'm ready." She wore a combination of the clothes she'd worn in the Cities and the ones she'd bought. Same old sweater but new leggings and boots.

Caleb was the same. Shiny hair slicked back, and the sides freshly shaved. Instead of a black T-shirt, he wore a red shirt emblazoned with a fire engine in red, white, and blue. She could pick him out of a crowd, but she'd always been able to do that.

Justin hopped in with them on the way into town. Caleb was driving his truck. Less conspicuous for Justin that way.

Brigit buckled herself in. "Not planning on making any more babies?" His situation was no joke, but she used humor to get Justin through these dark days.

Justin snorted. "Not in Moore anyway. I feel like I'd

endanger any woman I looked at." He was only half joking. "And I have to prove I'm a daddy in the first place."

The parking lot of the bar was packed. Caleb took a loop around looking for Maisy's car.

"I don't see it." Justin peered out the window. "I think we're good. For now."

"Let's go ring in the new year," she said. Her stomach fluttered. She hadn't been out much since returning to Moore. Once in a while, she'd gone out with Oliver and hated every minute. He'd been determined to play the golden boy come home again, when really they'd only moved back because it was the last option. And there was always the risk of running across Caleb and reminding herself of the heartbreak that never faded.

She and Caleb hadn't done more than grab a quick lunch or supper. They were both trying to save money and were perfectly content to curl up on the couch and watch TV.

Justin's troubles had only made her leery of running across Maisy's spies. She had a pack of them spreading lies in order to recruit townspeople to her side. It was a small town. Her friends and family would track and report Justin's whereabouts and who he was talking to.

Once they were out of the cold and in the loud bar, she spotted her cousin Aaron. His wife Dalisay was next to him and his friend Lucas sat across from them. When Aaron saw them, he waved them over.

Lucas stood to pull another table over.

Aaron gave her a hug. "I think we're the only Walkers going out to ring in the new year." He grinned at his wife's baby belly. "At least this year."

She smiled back, ecstatic for them. "You'll be glad to be stuck at home. How are Jackson and Nicolas?"

"Giving Mom more gray hair. Come on. Have a seat." He

didn't bat an eye when Caleb draped an arm over the back of her chair.

An hour of stories and gut-busting laughter flew by. Brigit had killed off a beer and a couple glasses of water. She leaned over to Caleb. "I need to use the restroom."

"Want another drink?"

"Yeah, I'll take another beer." All three of them were going light tonight. Caleb was driving, and Justin wanted to be prepared for a confrontation.

She got up to find the bathroom and he went to the bar. The night was fun, but she stayed in the bathroom stall a few extra minutes to soak up the muffled silence. There was a time when a noisy bar had been the best bar. It wasn't just Minneapolis. Her tastes had changed.

She must be getting old. Or too used to enjoying a quiet ranch.

After finishing, she headed out. Turning out of the hall-way, she nearly ran into the lone occupant of the first table outside the restroom entrance.

"Oh, Brigit." Maisy's painted red lips pursed.

Brigit tensed. The water she'd drunk churned in her stomach. God, she didn't want drama. "Hello, Maisy."

"I suppose Justin told you? You're going to be an aunt?"

Brigit almost glanced at the table they'd been sitting at, but maybe she had an icicle's chance in hell that Maisy hadn't noticed Justin was here. "I hear it's a possibility."

Irritation flushed Maisy's face. "It's more than a possibil-ity. I know who the father of my kid is."

"Right. You're feeling well then?" She wanted to run. To keep from giving away Justin's presence despite it being inevitable, she scanned the bar.

Priya, with her glossy black hair, her designer purse, and that damn med school degree was smiling at Caleb. Her hand was on her hip, and her head was tilted as if hanging on every word coming out of his mouth.

Maisy followed her gaze. "They make a cute couple."

The woman's smugness laced Brigit's spine with steel, but she wasn't going to feed the jealousy beast. "Caleb would look good with anyone."

"Especially Priya, though. She's so…petite." Maisy didn't even bother to look her up and down to make her point. She was too practiced at hitting her target.

Don't take the bait. "Yes, she's very cute. Excuse me." She attempted to sidle past, but Maisy's vise grip on her bicep stopped her.

"Tell Justin I need to talk to him."

"I'll let him know." She tugged on her arm.

Maisy's grip tightened to painful. "I'll just come with you."

"It's best if you don't."

"Maybe you didn't hear me around those hips of yours, Bridge. I'm coming with you."

At first the comment stung, like always. No. She'd had enough and didn't need to tolerate Maisy's insults. "Maisy, grow up. Comments about my weight were childish and immature when we were kids. They're still rude and petty. You have business with my brother? This isn't the time or the place. Now, I'm going to meet up with *my* boyfriend. He loves my hips."

Maisy's face turned stony. Fire flashed in her eyes, but there was enough sanity in her to know that what Brigit had said was true. Brigit gave her arm a little twist. Maisy snapped her hand back, her gaze assessing.

As Brigit barely managed not to run away, she couldn't help but wonder if she'd taught Maisy a lesson, or made the woman fortify her defenses.

Caleb's smile widened when she approached. The way he looked at her eased the constant anxiety she had being out with him. Her constant fear of being judged. They weren't teenagers anymore. And she'd finally spoken her mind to Maisy without stooping to her level.

Caleb pushed off the counter and held out her beer. When she took it, he tucked her into his side. His easy smile and friendly presence were in place.

Priya blinked and took a sip from her glass, her gaze bouncing between them.

Brigit swallowed her frustration with the fizz of her cold beer. *Why so surprised?*

Caleb tightened his arm as if sensing her need for a little extra support. "Priya here is Moore's newest OB/GYN."

"Wow. Congrats." Brigit reflected on herself. Nope. No jealousy.

Priya smiled, pride radiating from her. "I honestly thought I'd never reach this point. And come back home on top of it." She cocked her head. "Weren't you going to go to med school?"

Brigit studied the other women but detected no malice. Her tone was curious, not catty, unlike her friend Maisy. Had Priya been like that in school too? Had Brigit assumed the worst because of who Priya associated with?

"No, law school was my initial plan, but I changed my mind in college."

"Oh." Priya shrugged her delicate shoulders. "And here I saw you back in town and thought maybe there'd be two of us young docs charging into Moore Community Health and... Well." She gulped the rest of the liquid in her glass.

If Brigit could pick one girl from her past to vote Ms. Perfect, it'd be Priya. But the woman didn't chug her drink out of perfection. "Isn't your dad still a doctor there?"

"He is." Priya grimaced. "Which will come in handy when a colleague or patient wants to second-guess me. They can go straight to him."

"It'll take time," Caleb said. "We don't get too many new doctors, and it's gotta be hard in a town that remembers when you were in pigtails."

"Pri," Maisy's sharp voice cut it. "It's time to go." Maisy stalked away.

Brigit didn't miss the fortifying breath Priya took, nor the way she deliberately avoided looking at Maisy. Priya set her glass down and smiled at them, but her eyes brimmed with concern.

Brigit couldn't help but ask, "Is she…doing okay?"

Priya gripped her purse until her knuckles were white. "I've always felt like I should apologize for the way she acted, but I talked myself out of it. Now we're adults and she's *still* —" She shook her head. "Anyway, I'm so sorry, Brigit. For everything. I should've told her straight up to stop. Instead, I ran ahead of her and tried to minimize anything she'd find to pick on. Hindsight and all that. Anyway, it was great seeing you two and, uh, together."

Caleb gave her a little wave as she left, but he didn't steer Brigit back to their table. "That was unexpected."

"In so many ways." An old nemesis hadn't turned into a friend, but at least she was no longer an enemy. And she was someone Brigit could commiserate with. "I don't think her friendship with Maisy is in the same place it was ten years ago."

"Maisy might be in the same place, but the rest of us aren't."

The rest of us? That pool felt tiny. Maisy was the same, if not worse, and guys like Teddy treated her no differently than before. Moore hadn't changed, but Brigit had just stood up for herself. And not everyone in Moore insulted or somehow demeaned her. There were people like Priya, who was actually pleasant. Or had she always been that way, but Brigit had been too jaded to see it? The longer she stayed, the harder it was to see everything that Moore didn't offer.

THE FIRE ENGINE WAS WASHED, and its red exterior was shiny enough to see his face in. After the snowfall in the last week and the extra car accidents the weather had caused, it had needed a good cleaning.

"Apparatus looks good, Cruise." Tate McGill gathered the hoses.

"I can wash this thing in my sleep." Caleb helped Tate put all the cleaning supplies away.

"Was that Priya Patel I saw you talking up at the bar last weekend?"

"Yeah, but we're just friends."

"Right. I've heard the guys say something about Brigit Walker." Tate leaned against the apparatus.

Caleb scowled at him. He hadn't talked to his crew much about Brigit. Mostly because he didn't want to face all the questions and advice about when she got a job in a big city, not because he wasn't dying to talk about the woman who was the center of his world. "You're a nosy fucker, McGill."

The guy laughed, his boom filling the garage. "Brigit Walker it is, then. Congrats, man. You're finally seeing someone for more than one night."

"Nah. It's not that serious." His stomach twisted just saying it. "She's moving soon, once she gets a job."

Tate's smile faded. "That sucks. I mean, I thought since she was someone you were actually dating…"

Damn Tate and the way he seemed to see through all their bullshit. "If I could have my way."

A voice crackled over the intercom. "Cruise. Come to my office."

"The LT wants to talk to you. What'd you do?" Tate chuckled. "Kidding. But seriously, you're not trapped here. You're a firefighter with experience. If she's worth having, don't let her get away."

It wasn't up to him whether she left or not, and he couldn't make her ask him to come with.

Caleb jogged to his lieutenant's office, rolling through everything he'd done. He'd seen the fire chief walking through earlier, too, but he was on good terms with the man. They used to be neighbors, but now the chief's sons ran the ranch. Not long ago, there had been trouble between Caleb and them, but that had been resolved. One of the silver linings of the tornado.

The office came into view. Chief Bradford sat in one of the chairs across from the LT's desk.

Caleb nodded to him as he entered. "Chief." He glanced at Lieutenant Johnson. "Sir."

"Have a seat, Cruise."

Nerves rippled in his gut. His butt hit the chair and he settled his hands on his legs. He couldn't lose this job. A firefighter with experience was no good if he'd been fired.

LT did all the talking. "Cortez put in his resignation."

Cortez was one of their driver engineers. He and Caleb didn't work together often, but he'd heard talk that Cortez's wife had gotten a promotion that'd take them to the East Coast. But what did that have to do with him?

"So that means we have an opening. And Lieutenant Mills is talking retirement."

Caleb had heard the same, but he'd been too distracted with planning ways to afford his house and get more income out of his ranch to dwell on it.

The chief cut in. "What are your plans for the future, Caleb?" The chief had a way of treating all of them like sons.

Maybe that was why his owns sons had resented Caleb, but that was water out of the hose.

"I'm working on my emergency management degree." He loved both of his jobs. "My plans are to stick with the department. I love my job."

LT rested his elbows on his desk. "And we'd like you to stay. We'd also like to see you move up. Have you given thought to continuing your education so you'll qualify for these openings as they happen?"

"I did. Before the storm." With sheer fortitude, he'd continued with his college courses. Both to feel like he was still moving forward, and because, like the LT had said, he needed to keep thinking about his future.

The other guys nodded, knowing exactly which storm he meant.

"You have a lot on your plate, Cruise," LT said. "However we can help, let us know. But I'd like to see your name in the pool of applicants for driver engineer."

That driver engineer position would be one rung up the ladder. One step closer to lieutenant. He'd been working here long enough to start considering promotions. Hadn't he been telling himself that he was a firefighter with experience?

The chief's gruff voice interrupted his thoughts. "We're not in our twenties forever. Sometimes, it's the back that goes. Or our knees. Or we have an accident, illness, what have you. My point is, you gotta start planning now for when you're older and can't haul hoses and crawl up ladders anymore. And a promotion won't hurt the checkbook."

Reality sank in as he calculated the starting wage for a driver engineer. If he got the job, he could approach the bank again. On that salary, he could afford a higher mortgage even without widening the income and expense gap of the ranch.

And if he could build on that income, he'd be set for when he was promoted again.

LT tapped the desk. "Why don't I email you the job qualifications and all the information I have on continuing ed? If you have any questions, hit me up, anytime."

"Thank you, sir." He nodded again to Chief Bradford. "Chief. Thank you."

"You were always a hard-working kid, Caleb," the chief said. "I would hate to lose you."

Caleb frowned once he left LT's office. Had they heard he was seeing Brigit and that she was planning to move? Did the whole town think he'd go with her?

The whole town except her.

CHAPTER 14

*B*rigit trailed her fingers over the mouse pad on her laptop. The page on the screen was open to jobs in Arizona. Close to her parents.

She'd exhausted places in Minneapolis that she was qualified for, but that damn lack of experience—relevant experience. At this rate, her sleazy ex qualified for more jobs than she did because of his insurance background.

She knew practically no one else in other major cities, and moving somewhere and starting over was no longer appealing. How times had changed.

At night, she slept with Caleb in his room, but during the day, she applied for jobs in here. She was isolating this part of herself away from the fun she had with Caleb. This damn computer shadowed her relationship with Caleb.

She slept with him. Ate with him. Did chores with him. But they weren't moving forward, not as a couple.

There was nowhere for her to go. She was happy, for now, but she couldn't continue to rely on Caleb, Justin, and her parents to support her through life.

Clicking to her other screen, she scowled at the dismal

list of positions in Moore. Night clerk at the bigger hotel in town. Gas station attendant. Nurses. She should've gone to nursing school. There were always openings, and they actually paid a livable wage. Unlike the gas station and night clerk. The benefits in those places helped, but not enough.

Besides, the only creatures she wanted to nurse had cloven hoofs. Maybe she should've set her sights on veterinary school. But no. Then she would've been a full-time vet watching everyone else ranch. Might as well make a clean break.

Only it wouldn't be clean anymore, would it?

Caleb.

He'd gotten home from work this morning and run out to his place to check on things. *I'll bring home lunch. I have to talk with you about work.*

Her work, or his? He hadn't said, but he seemed part excited and part stressed.

Closing the window for Moore's classifieds, she prepared herself to search Phoenix's openings. Hell, maybe she should look at Fargo. It was big enough and constantly growing. But it was also far enough away that a commute wasn't ideal, and she'd be caught between wanting to move home and not being able to. She'd also be close enough to learn about how everyone else moved on with their lives once she left.

Caleb.

Her heart twisted. What was she going to do?

The phone rang.

She saw the number and sucked in a breath. This was the call she'd been waiting for.

Shaking her hands, she blew out, "Hello?"

"Hi. Can I talk to Brigit Walker, please?"

Brigit recognized the department manager she'd interviewed with in Minneapolis. Her smile grew until her cheeks hurt. "This is Brigit."

Finally, a little validation that she'd done well, that all her hard studying over the years would amount to something. That *she'd* amounted to something.

"Hi, Brigit. This is Danielle Costa with Golden Waves Credit Union. Listen, you're going to be getting a letter from us, but I wanted to contact you in person."

Brigit wiggled. The impending move, uprooting herself to move back to the city, and leaving her loved ones behind all took a backseat to this moment. She'd give herself this moment to celebrate a hard-won victory.

Danielle continued. "I was just so impressed with you, but unfortunately I wasn't the only person involved in the decision." Brigit's smile wavered and faded the more Danielle spoke. "The position was offered to another applicant and they accepted. I wanted to call personally and thank you for coming out to speak with us, and I urge you to apply with us again."

"Oh… Okay." Her vision blurred, and she dropped her head into her free hand. "Thanks for calling."

Danielle said a few other things, but Brigit didn't catch them. She just wanted to get off the phone and break down. She managed to say goodbye and sound semiprofessional.

Foolish, foolish, foolish. Why would the best place out of all the ones she'd applied to offer her a spot when she could barely get her resume taken seriously anywhere else?

Tears rolled down her cheeks. All that school for nothing. Mom and Dad had paid for all that school and she couldn't use it. Oliver had carried her ass for years while she'd gotten her degrees. *He* had a job.

All she had to show were snail mail and digital letters of rejection.

Time ticked by. She sighed and went to the bathroom. Hopefully a little water would take some of the puffiness out of her face.

Trudging back into her bedroom, she settled in with her laptop. What jobs were open in Phoenix again?

Time ticked by and she moved on from devastated to numb. By now, she had a process to applying. Need a resume? She had three different types. References? Three to five, take your pick. List of addresses, all the schools she'd attended, it was all at her fingertips.

By the time a motor droned closer and closer to the house, she'd put in for five different positions in Phoenix. Two market research analysts, an operations research analyst, and—to hell with it—a clinic administrator.

Getting on her coat and stepping into her boots, she resolved to be cool and collected. She wasn't sure if she could tell the story without tears, and while Caleb was always her cheerleader, showing her in so many ways that he had complete faith in her, he shouldn't have to do it constantly.

Yes, not getting this job was a big deal, but it was a bump in the road and she'd wait until she could hold the water-works at bay.

Outside, Caleb was at the shop, brushing a dusting of snow off the cement slab in front of the main door.

He looked up, squinting in the bright sun of a winter day. "Hey. Hungry?"

"I think there's some leftover venison from last night in the fridge."

"Want to go to town?"

Not really, but it'd do her good to get out. Face her disappointment and keep going. "Sure."

She looked down at her favorite pair of jeans that were nearly white around the knees. The coat she'd chosen was her Carhartt Sherpa-lined jacket. It'd seen more than a few chore days and while she washed it often, its natural state was now grunge.

"You look fine. We'll just hit the Brown House."

Her stomach growled at the thought of their greasy burger and fries. The day hovered above zero degrees and doing chores in the cold always ramped up her appetite.

He kept pushing snow. The dusting was closer to an inch, and while Justin didn't need much of an excuse to fire up the snow blower, her brother was with Maisy at one of her first OB appointments. With Priya as the OB. He'd either want to work until he dropped when he got back or collapse on the couch with a six-pack.

There was always something to do. Brigit grabbed the big shop broom and joined Caleb.

"Anything exciting happen today?" Breath puffed out of the coat collar he'd crunched his face in to block the wind.

She liked the sting. It reminded her that she had a warm bed to go to each night and a family that loved and supported her. A little below-zero wind chill centered her. "I found out I didn't get the job we went to the Cities for."

Damn. She hadn't meant to spill it so soon. But this was as good a place to talk as any. Any tears would disappear in the cold, dry air, and it'd look like the weather was the reason her eyes watered.

"Shit, Bridge. I'm sorry."

She stopped pushing the broom, both hands gripping the handle. "They liked me enough to call and tell me to keep applying. Not sure how to interpret that."

"That's good, right?"

"Better than nothing." She was about to tell him that she'd applied to several places in Phoenix, but she ducked her head and plowed another strip clear.

"And Moore's still..."

"I looked and didn't find anything," she said, her tone shorter than she'd intended. Was that guilt rearing its head? She was enjoying her time with Caleb. But getting a job meant leaving him. It was a weird contradiction she lived in.

"We should eat before the lunch rush hits, or everyone's going to listen to what we say."

Caleb glanced at the house, his expression pensive.

"What?"

"We don't have to—"

"I didn't get shitty news to have leftovers. Come on. Justin paid me for last week. I'll treat." Caleb lifted his shovel but didn't move. "The LT called me into the office. They want me to apply for a position that's opening soon. It'll mean more responsibility but more pay. And it's a stepping stone to future promotions."

The cold wasn't so refreshing now. It sapped her energy, chapped her cheeks, and she wanted to crawl under the covers. Caleb didn't want to shake salt on her wounded pride and was offering to let her stay home and sulk. He was also stifling his own good news for her.

"Then we definitely need to eat out." Her words came out too cheerful, but dammit, she was trying.

"Bridge—"

"Caleb. You're good at your job. You're trying to build a house. This is good news. Don't hide it because you think I'll feel bad."

He closed the distance between them and stood so he blocked the wind. "How you feel is important to me."

He was a good man. The best. His grandparents should get a commendation. "And your good news is important to me."

His gaze swept over her face. "You always have a place with me." The corner of his lips popped up. "Well, when I have a place." He grew serious. "But my ranch is your ranch. I think the cows listen to you better."

It almost sounded like he was proposing. Oh God, what would she say? Elation nearly pushed all thought aside.

No, of course he wasn't proposing. He wasn't the type of guy to ask her to marry him just to get her to stay.

Even if she wanted to stay. Was she strong enough to face the uphill battle of being a rancher's wife? A life of insisting that she didn't have to defer to Caleb because she was in charge? Would she really be in charge? Was there such a thing as a pity ranch?

Regardless, she didn't need to figure it out now. "We should get going."

His jaw tensed. She'd stepped on his feelings, but analyzing them out in the cold wouldn't help either of them. Especially when her single-minded goal for the last ten years was in danger of evaporating with her tears.

CHAPTER 15

Caleb scowled into his beer. The bar was quiet tonight. One of the perks of having an odd schedule. He wasn't restricted to Friday and Saturday nights, when it was too loud to talk. And he was at the age where he went to a bar to *talk*. Women weren't on his agenda anymore. Not until this thing with Brigit died a slow painful death, which was the only outcome he could foresee.

"It's been a few months now," Jesse said. The guy refused Caleb's money so all he could do was buy as many drinks—Sprite in Jesse's case—and meals as he could. Jesse reached for a slice of the pizza they were splitting. "You and Brigit must be pretty serious."

"Yeah, you'd think." One of them was serious. He was afraid the other was biding her time.

"It's February and you two still seem to be a thing."

Caleb could rattle off the exact date Brigit had moved in, but that'd just look pathetic. "She's heading to Phoenix for a job interview. Research market analyst. Market research analyst? Whatever."

"Sounds exciting." Jesse leveled him with a stare. He

didn't have to push to get Caleb talking. It wasn't like he could go to Justin with these issues. He probably could, but Justin had ninety-nine problems. Caleb wasn't going to be one of them.

"I've offered her my ranch, told her she could live with me. But she wants a job."

"You proposed?" Thankfully, Jesse kept his voice down. There might not be a lot of people here, but it only took one with acute hearing to spread rumors that'd send Brigit running.

"No, I didn't propose. I just…tossed the option out there." He'd offered himself up as a possibility for her future. And she'd said they should go eat.

At least she wasn't leading him on and making promises she didn't plan to keep. Nope. She was applying out of state.

As if sensing that this discussion wasn't the most uplifting, Jesse switched topics. "Farah's dad gave you the award for best Christmas present ever."

His mood lifted. Or he could pretend it did. "He liked the deer sausage?"

"Loved it. He hasn't gone hunting since before Corinne's stroke."

His phone buzzed. The usual spike of excitement hit. Was it Brigit? He'd had to work yesterday when she'd flown out, and he couldn't help but wonder if she'd planned it that way. A little awkward to ask your boyfriend for a ride to the airport for a job that'd probably tank the relationship. But whatever.

But when he saw the caller, his heart sank. Shit. "I'll be right back."

Jesse nodded as Caleb rose and answered, "What's up, Mom?"

"Where are you?"

Hello to you too. "I'm in Moore."

She cackled, the years of smoking obvious. "Smart-ass. Where at in town? I'll swing by and see you."

Mom was in town? Thanksgiving and Christmas had come and gone without so much as a text or email. She probably didn't realize Valentine's Day was next week. "Just you or is—"

"Fuck, no. I dumped his ass, but Randall's with me and I want to show him the farm."

"Who?" Dumped Russ's ass? But Russ had been the one constant in Mom's life. The guy had been halfway decent to Caleb. He'd been the one to drag Mom to his high school graduation on time. And he'd answered his phone when Mom had lost or refused to answer her own. "What happened between you and Russ?"

"It doesn't matter now. You'll like Randall. He's a cowboy too."

Right. There was a difference between a guy who called himself a cowboy and a guy who actually worked the land and animals for a living. Those weren't the types of guys Mom was attracted to though. She gravitated toward the men who might wear the boots, even the hat, but preferred hanging out in a bar for a living.

"I'm off tomorrow. I can take you both out and show you around."

"*Psst.* Caleb, I can still find my home."

But it's not yours. And there's not a home there right now. "I don't want you around there at night. It's too easy to get hurt."

"Caleb, I'm an adult and your mother, and that is my home. If I wanna take Randall there and show him around, I'm gonna do it."

His grandparents had made sure the land, the house, the finances—all of it was in his name and his name only. They loved Mom, but they'd had the foresight and the fortitude to make sure she couldn't interfere with Caleb's future any more than she had. As for the ranch? Mom didn't give two shits about the cattle or how to keep them alive.

Arguing with Mom was pointless. She didn't see her own faults. Everyone else was to blame.

"If you're going out tonight, I can meet you there." *And make sure you don't plow down a fence taking a wrong turn into an approach.* "Where are you staying in town?"

She laughed again and dissolved into a fit of coughing. "We'll stay at the house, silly Billy."

He no longer warmed at the pet name. It was a smoke-screen. Her way of making him and everyone else think she cared much more than she did. But her words hammered the last nails on the lid of "Mom only cares about herself" box. "The house was demolished last year, Mom. Remember? The tornado?"

"What the fuck are you talking about?"

"I sent you a message. And a picture after the house was demolished."

"When?"

"Last summer. The big tornado that went through Moore and over my place." Had stressing *my* been too obvious? Probably not if his message of "a tornado flattened the house" and a photo of a big gaping hole where their family home used to be hadn't gotten the point across.

"And you didn't fucking call? Caleb, my house is gone and you didn't even call?"

"I tried, but it just rang."

"That's right. I lost my phone and got another one. Must've been during that time."

It was plausible. Mom was always losing her phone and getting new ones, and she was on her third phone number in five years. It was the one time he hadn't called Russ when Mom went into radio silence. Life had been too crazy for

Caleb at the time. If he'd gotten ahold of Russ, he might've learned about the breakup.

A gusty sigh traveled over the line. "I dragged Randall all the way here and there's nothing to show him. Story of my life."

Caleb squeezed his eyes shut. Nothing to show Randall? Mom had dragged her new man here to see a house that she'd barely spent any time in once she'd turned eighteen.

"Yeah, it sucks. I've been living at Justin's."

"The Walkers? Do they make you cook and clean?"

"I cook and clean up after myself because Justin's letting me stay there for free." Why did he bother arguing? Mom would think what she wanted. He searched for a subject change—and a way to keep them from driving through his yard in the dark. Mom wasn't known for passing up getting behind the wheel after she'd had a few. "Want to meet me out there tomorrow? I can show you what the tornado did, and you can see what it looks like without a house."

"I guess we'll have to get a motel." She couldn't sound more inconvenienced. "Yeah, why don't we do that? We'll check out, grab lunch, and see you about one o'clock."

There was no *yeah, I'd like to see you, son, it's been awhile* or *why don't you meet us for lunch,* but she'd agreed to meet, and he couldn't deny the little boy inside of him wanting to see his mother.

It shouldn't be this warm in winter.

Brigit stepped through the revolving glass door and squinted into the sun. Traffic buzzed over the busy street that ran in front of the office center she'd just interviewed in. Heels clacked on the concrete from passersby. Many were dressed in business attire more expensive than what she'd donned, and others were dressed like she would be at home right now. A sweater and jeans.

When she'd arrived in Phoenix two days ago, she'd had to go shopping yet again. Her sweater dress might've worked, but for a Minnesota girl suddenly finding herself in temps in the lower seventies in the middle of winter, she would've been red-faced and sweaty while she met with her prospective employers.

Market research analyst.

The job sounded…not exciting. Deskbound. Full of water-cooler conversations and reheated leftovers eaten under bright fluorescent lights. Hours staring at a computer screen. While they'd covered what her duties would be if she landed the job and given her a tour of cubicle hell, she'd questioned what the hell she'd been thinking when she'd gone to business school. What else had she thought a business job would entail?

Her heels mingled with the rest of the foot traffic as she hustled to a coffee shop on the next block over. Once inside, she rattled off the same low-fat, low-carb drink she always used to get. While waiting, she sent Dad a message. Mom hadn't been able to ask for time off. But she must enjoy the job. Most couples her parents' age moved to Arizona to retire and escape the bone-aching cold, but Mom had scored a decent job and often commented on the benefits. Dad sold used cars and never complained either. Maybe it was the promise of a steady paycheck, or maybe retirement equaled boredom for them, or maybe the change in climate was enough.

Her drink was ready. She threaded through the full tables, out the door, to the side street Dad had arranged to pick her up on. Taking a cautious sip, she wrinkled her nose as ultra-sweetened nonfat coated her tongue. Blech. How quickly her taste buds had adjusted to real cream and sugar. Each drink reminded her that skinny wasn't always as good as great-tasting food.

Nursing the cup just for something to do, she was happy to trash it when Dad pulled up.

"Hey, kiddo. Mind if I drop you off at home and head back to work? A guy's gone today, and they need me on deck."

"No problem." Her heart sank. Adulthood snuck up on her at the most unexpected times. She was in Arizona, staying off the beaten path with her parents, but she hadn't been able to spend that much time with them. It was like the holidays provided too much time, but without their vacation days, there wasn't much time for visiting.

She watched the city go by, seemingly identical stucco home after stucco home, on the way to the house and chatted about the weather and what they planned for supper. Dad let her into the house and took off.

Brigit changed into plaid pajama pants and a T-shirt. No car. Not ambitious enough to brave public transportation. And bored. She padded through the house. Where would she live if she moved here? An apartment? A condo? Would she eventually buy a stucco home with a ceramic tile floor and a pool? She glanced around. Done all in beige?

This was a nice place, and much newer than her family home. But it looked like every other house in the development. Mom had added her own touches, and some that were obviously Dad's, but there was nothing to suggest Mom and Dad used to live in the country on a ranch.

She missed those touches. The photos of their own horses grazing in the pastures. The aerial view of the property. And especially artwork of the prairie countryside.

She would miss all of that. Having her own place in a cubicle farm held no appeal. It was one thing if the work appealed to her, but it didn't. At all. There was nothing about nature in this type of work. She wouldn't have any reason to keep up on cattle feed trends, or work with Justin on which colostrum worked better for his lambs, or have a hand in Caleb lowering the open rates of his cows.

Already, her mind fit ideas into place. Start with mineral. Change silage from corn to sorghum. Research another bull to purchase to breed in heartier DNA.

But here, she'd get farther and farther out of touch with the industry the longer she was working behind plated glass on the fifth floor of an office building.

Digging out her phone, she called Caleb. When he answered, she briefly closed her eyes. Hearing his voice was a balm to irritations she hadn't known existed.

"Hey," she said. "Interview's done."

"How'd it go?" His words were taken by the wind. A car door opening and closing was muffled over the line.

"It went well. Did I catch you at a bad time?"

"Nope. I might have to go when my mom arrives, though."

"Your mom's in town?" She hated that she couldn't be there for him. She'd always thought of his mom as a petite natural disaster. She rolled into town, caused some sort of devastation—usually with her own son—and left for an unknown, often extended, amount of time.

"With a new dude. I guess Russ kicked her out."

"I'm sorry."

"It is what it is." There was Caleb's eternal tolerance for his mom's behavior. Her own mom saw it as a failure of his, but not Brigit. It was self-preservation. Anger and bitterness at Adele would only hurt him, not her. "They wanted to see the place so I'm meeting them out here."

"I'll let you go then."

"You don't have to. They're not here yet." The edge in his voice was unmistakable.

"When is she supposed to get there?"

"Twenty minutes ago." Ouch. "So, the interview? How'd it really go?"

"The interview? Perfect. They seemed happy with me. The job, though…"

"That bad?"

"No. It'd be okay for someone who was into that kind of work. I don't know if I'm cut out for it." She almost whispered. But no one was home. Just she and Caleb knew the truth.

"You've always liked to get your hands dirty, literally. You were born and raised a rancher, Bridge. It's okay to do that for a living. It's okay to *want* to do that for a living."

"I think I'm realizing that now." Her breath froze. That was a hell of an admission.

"You'd be willing to stay in Moore. With me?" The awe in his voice warmed her more than the Phoenix sun ever could.

"I've grudgingly started seeing Moore's appeal." She'd stood up to Maisy. Priya wasn't the mean-girl monster she recalled. Seeing her twin everyday was more than a bonus, and living close to her other brother and his family was something she'd missed more than she thought.

And dammit, like that credit union in Minneapolis thought, she was educated and experienced. The Teddies of Moore would just have to deal with her. She'd make sure of it.

"And you're in Moore," she said.

"Then come home. We'll figure it out. You and I."

A smile tugged at her lips. "My flight's tomorrow, anyway." She was going home. Home. Phoenix wasn't her home, and she didn't have to make it be her home.

"I know. It sucks waking up without you." And he'd said his ranch was her ranch.

"Can I do this? Can I really do this?" Was she brave

enough to change a life's worth of expectations to spend her time with the man she loved? She hadn't told him she loved him. But she'd rectify that when she got back.

"You want to do it, Brigit. We'll make it happen."

"Twenty-four hours and I'll be home." They disconnected. She had to stare at the phone for a while. She'd just made plans to stay in Moore. To stay with Caleb and use the animal science degree she'd snuck into her coursework.

And it felt right. So, so right.

She grinned and squealed, pumping her arms and wiggling her hips. Tonight, she'd talk to Mom and Dad. It might be a heavy conversation, but a long, long overdue one.

So... What now?

She no longer had to hop online and go through more classifieds. Watch TV?

That wasn't appealing. Too much anticipation flowed through her veins. Her dream job was at her fingertips. But she couldn't just pace the hard floor until Mom and Dad came home.

Did Dad still subscribe to ranching magazines? A guy who'd ranched as long as him couldn't just drop it. Over the last year, she'd avoided all her favorite reads on agriculture trends and animal practices. All her stuff had been online, but Dad was old-fashioned. Maybe she could find something to page through while dreaming about her wide-open future.

Ooh—maybe she could write for a magazine like that. Start her own blog. People made money off those, right? She could figure it out.

Thinking outside the box was easy when that box had been busted wide open. All those ideas banging around in her head—workshops, presentations at ag conventions, or even just short seminars for farmers and ranchers in her own area. None of her education would go to waste.

It'd take time to build toward profitability, but with Caleb's help, she had time. They had time. Together.

She entered the second bedroom that functioned as an office and catchall room. Bookshelves flanked the desk. Perusing the first shelf didn't unearth anything she was dying to read, and the *Farm & Ranch* mags stacked on the second shelf she'd already read.

"Where's the new stuff, Dad?" she muttered. She might have to look on his nightstand.

As she turned to round the desk, her thigh hit a pile of papers. They fluttered to the floor.

"Damn."

Squatting, she swept them into a pile and was in the middle of straightening them out when she stopped. These were tax documents, and the pile included correspondence with their accountant.

Brigit sifted through them. Withdrawals from their retirement account over the years had all her attention. Calculations about catch up and how much longer they'd have to work to make up for the difference knocked her on her ass. She folded her legs under her and read through the documents.

Her parents had paid for her school. All of it. She'd assumed they'd saved for her and her siblings' college tuitions, but they hadn't really. Travis's, maybe. But being hit with twins and saving enough to get them both through school after the firstborn had gotten not only a degree, but a PhD, had tapped them out.

Her parents weren't working to stave off the boredom of retirement. They didn't have enough to retire.

Tears welled in her eyes. Her parents were broke and hadn't told anyone. And they were broke because of her.

Her phone rang. She stared at it numbly. An unknown number.

"Hello," she answered woodenly.

"Brigit Walker?"

"Yes." She had no desire to be pleasant.

"Hi, this is Emily from Murphy and Associates. We'd like to meet with you about the operations analyst position. Are you available early next week for an interview?"

Early next week? She had a flight home tomorrow. Into Caleb's waiting arms. She was supposed to tell her parents about what she really wanted to do with her life. But they were working. Because they'd spent all their money on her education.

"Yes, I can meet with you next week."

AS THE WAIT GREW LONGER, his only solace was tomorrow. Brigit would be home tomorrow, and they could start planning their future together. He could rely on Brigit. Apparently not his own mom. But then he knew that.

Then why, after an hour, was he still waiting, wasting his gas as he idled in the driveway on his property? He should've dressed for work, but he thought he'd come here and give his mom and her new man a tour. A new man. Caleb had stupidly wanted to make a good impression and see if the man measured up at all to the man he called Dad. Russ had never earned being called Dad, but dammit.

Caleb took one more looked around his property. He'd messaged Mom a few times, but she hadn't replied.

He heaved a heavy breath and called her.

"Yeah?" she answered in her raspy voice.

"Hey, Mom. Weren't you going to meet me and look around?"

"Oh that. It's cold and this town ain't got nothing for me. I don't even know why I came back."

Really? There's nothing in this town for you? Not one thing that's walking and talking, that you birthed yourself? But he'd had an hour for the real reason to dawn on him. Mom's new man had heard stories of profitable land with a house. He wanted to see for himself and scam his way into it. If the guy was anything like Mom, free money and a rent-free place to live were as intoxicating as the alcohol and cigarettes she loved so much. But no house and an adult son proved too many complications.

Wasn't that why Russ had stuck around before he'd gotten sucked into Mom's vortex so far he couldn't get out until she'd done the unthinkable to him two or three times?

What would Grandma say? *Her actions are for her alone. Don't take no responsibility for them.* Followed by the unspoken thought he heard from her loud and clear: *Because she ain't taking responsibility for you.*

But damn, it stung. The woman who was always supposed to have his back had let him down over and over again. She always chose him last, if she chose him at all.

Made a guy feel wanted.

But tomorrow, Brigit was coming home. And he wouldn't leave her waiting at an airport for an hour before he left her high and dry.

Mom was muttering something about good-for-nothing Moore when Caleb snapped back into the conversation.

"Nothing in Moore, Mom? I haven't seen you for years, but you come to town and go to the bar."

She was instantly defensive. "I never know your work schedule."

"You can ask. Sorry there's no house for you and what's-his-name to crash in, but even when I get a house built, you won't be welcome. Because here's my warning, Mom. Any of your guys step foot on *my* property, I'll call the police. And we both know they're right next door." And the other half of the reason Mom hadn't hung around when he was growing up.

"Well, listen to you," she sneered. "Just like your grandparents. You picked them over me, so don't expect me to come crying to you about *nothing*."

"I was a kid. I needed more than getting forgotten in a burning house while you and some random guy made it outside in your drunken stupor."

Swear words ripped over the line, but he disconnected. His heart hammered. He draped his arms over the steering wheel and laid his head in the middle. What a mess.

Had he just cut his mom out of his life? Would this be permanent?

Would he know the difference? Aside from the occasional birthday text and one Christmas card he could remember, Mom was a blank spot in his life. But he'd lied to himself about it. He'd lived with the hope that one day he'd wake up and have a mom like his friends and coworkers talked about. A pushy mom who got too far into his business because she cared so much about him. A mom he could confide in. A mom who came to town to see her son.

Somewhere along the line, he'd given up on the dad side. He mostly used the moniker to blend in, not because it gave him any real hope that Russ would suddenly act like one.

Maybe he should've done this before he lost his grandparents. Then he wouldn't feel so alone.

He had Brigit. And Justin. But their parents wouldn't welcome him into the fold. More likely, they'd blame him for fucking up Brigit's well-laid plans.

How would her talk go with them?

He kicked the pickup into gear and drove back to Justin's. As he was pulling in, his phone rang.

He dreaded seeing who the caller was. Mom wouldn't be calling to apologize. If it was her, it was to rip into him again.

Nope. It was work.

"Cruise," he answered.

"It's LT. I'm calling to tell you that you got the position."

Caleb parked in his spot and relaxed in his seat. "Thank you, sir." He'd needed this boost.

"You earned it. We'll talk specifics when you work next. Congratulations, Cruise. You impressed even me, and I've worked with you since the day you started. You're good at your job, but you can go as far as you want in this field. Remember that."

"Yes, sir." His work family had picked up the slack for his personal one. Between them and the Jameses, he'd be fine.

He went inside. Justin wasn't around, but the fridge actually had food in it. Caleb prepped supper, tossed it in the oven, and did some quick cleaning while it was cooking.

Justin came in like he had a sixth sense about when food was ready. The latter half of today had reminded Caleb of the days before Brigit moved back. Mellow. Congenial. Kind of boring.

Justin grabbed the plates when they were done. "I got the dishes. Did you vacuum?"

"And dusted."

"Damn, dude. I might have to marry you."

Caleb chuckled and went up to his room. He couldn't stand the wait. He sent Brigit a message. *Have you talked to them yet?*

An hour went by before his phone rang.

He answered, craving the sound of her voice. As long as he had her in his life, he could take whatever life threw his way. "Hey, Bridge."

"I talked to them." Her voice was heavy. Like she was fighting tears or had been crying.

He sat up. "What's wrong?"

"I'm, uh, not coming home tomorrow. I have another interview on Monday."

"But I thought—"

"They spent all their retirement putting me through school." Soft sobs carried over the line. "All of it. They're broke."

He tried to process what she was saying. "Your parents?"

"Yes. They had money saved for Travis. Justin's school didn't cost as much because he didn't sneak in all the extra classes. Then I went to graduate school. And added in more classes, more expenses. God, Caleb, I was so selfish."

"You weren't selfish. They're your parents."

"They can't retire. They wouldn't have enough to last more than five years."

The magnitude of what she said sank in. Joan and Rick had never let on that they were having financial trouble. Each time Justin asked, they claimed to love Arizona and their new jobs. They'd joke about working until they were seventy. But it wasn't a joke. They couldn't afford to quit. They'd worked their entire lives and raised three kids and sunk all their money into them.

Caleb had mad respect for parents willing to do that for their kids. But... Brigit wasn't coming back tomorrow? Another interview?

"Didn't you talk to them about what you really want to do with your life?" Seriously. Another interview? For a soul-crushing job that she had zero interest in?

She dropped to a ragged whisper. "How can I? I can't tell them they spent every last cent on my education and I'm not going to use it."

"What, like any old dumbass can ranch?"

"You know I don't mean that. But it won't pay them back like an office job here. I could live with them and—and work for a few years and help them out."

"Brigit, you're one of three kids who they helped through college. All this responsibility is not on your shoulders."

"Travis has a family. Justin…well, he has his situation. And they'd die before they let the guys know how much they were hurting financially. I barely got it out of them and if I hadn't found the papers on their desk, they wouldn't have told me."

"Because they want you to go and live the life you want for yourself."

"How can I do that, Caleb?"

He paused for a moment and squeezed his eyes shut. "So you're not coming home?"

"Not until next week."

"And then what?"

"I don't know. Move back when I get a job?"

"And us?" His anger was rising. Cold descended over him and he was transported back to that frigid wait for a mom who never came.

"I mean… I thought you'd understand."

"I think I understand all too well."

Just a few hours ago, he wouldn't have believed it either. But he was done waiting on people who only took from him.

"It wouldn't be for forever. I figured it out. I could pay them back, and in a few years, I could move back." She rushed on as if she sensed his walls going up. "We can do long-distance. Won't you wait for me?"

The word *wait* triggered his temper. "I waited for you for ten years, Brigit. I waited while you were in serious relationships with other men, and I waited while you lived the city life you thought you should have. I've done nothing but wait. I'm done waiting."

"Caleb, I don't understand—"

"I'm done waiting on people who can't be bothered with me. You didn't even ask if I could come with. My job is versatile. But just like in the Cities, you couldn't stand to be seen with me." The burn of shame didn't temper his ire.

"What are you talking about? I wanted to enjoy my time with you and not shout over the crowd. I wanted to go home with you."

"And you made sure that happened the second your interview was done."

Her silence on the other end was excruciating. "You know that's not how I think of you. You're important to me."

"Right. Just not enough."

She dragged in a breath he felt down to his toes. "I would think that a man who claims to love me would understand this situation. Or is it something else? Is the reality of me different than the fantasy and now you're pissed? We're not kids anymore with the luxury to dream about what we want to be when we grow up. I'm sorry I hurt you before, but this is totally different."

"No, it's not. It's just another tether your mom is using to get you to do her bidding."

"For fuck's sake, Caleb. She's not the wicked witch of the west. She's working. Everyday. And sometimes weekends. She's not sitting out here plotting how to break us up."

"Turns out she didn't have to," he snapped. This wasn't the conversation he'd thought he'd have tonight. This wasn't how he'd thought things would end between them. And for so long, he'd been sure they'd end. Their fling was temporary, and he'd gone in with eyes wide open. And hope. Always hope.

But then so much of his life had turned out better than he could've ever expected. He couldn't have it all, and he should've known that he and Brigit were never meant to be.

No matter how right it felt when he was with her.

CHAPTER 16

It was only the beginning of March. She started work tomorrow. A new job. The position she'd flown to Arizona to apply for. Her work outfits were purchased—all discount or on sale and from her own meager savings that she'd built working for Justin.

Forty- to fifty-hour workweeks. Benefits. Cubicles. Concrete. Ugh.

Justin said a winter storm was winding down. The sheep were okay and weren't lambing yet, but the temperature was still below zero with winds that could "shear the sheep itself."

If she were at home, she'd curse every time she had to go outside, but there was that slight rush of adrenaline. The thrill of getting her duties done in extreme conditions. The end-of-the-day feeling of accomplishment and the delicious fatigue in her body from using it for what she'd been born to do.

Brigit sat on her bed and tucked the phone to her ear. She called Justin one last time before the hectic week started. Never mind that she was incredibly homesick.

"A buyer came down from Fergus Falls and grabbed the

entire dining room set, even that heavy-ass hutch." Justin had graciously offered to sell off the heavy furniture that was more her mom's taste than anyone else's in the family.

"Thanks. You can send the money to Mom and Dad."

The bedroom set and living room pieces had already been sold. Only her clothing was left, and much of it she didn't fit into anyway. It was in a size she never planned to attain again, and she'd given Justin her blessing to donate it. All of it.

"I posted the wall decor."

"Thanks, Justin. I really mean it."

"Hey, it keeps me busy. I need that these days."

Yes. Her niece or nephew. Justin was uncomfortably confident that the baby was his. According to Priya, Maisy hadn't been seeing anyone and wasn't the type to sleep with a guy she wasn't in a relationship with—especially with Justin living in Moore. The insinuation was there that Maisy's obsession with him had made her want to be available if he ever even thought about calling her up again. And the rest was history.

"Still, you shouldn't have to deal with my belongings too." It was on the tip of her tongue to ask about Caleb. She only had to stop herself every five seconds.

Part of her was so damn angry with him. She wanted him to be aching and suffering as much as she was. But the other part of her wanted to know he was doing well.

"You're my twin." He gave a derisive laugh. "Caleb is my best friend, and you're both doing frustratingly well at keeping me out of the middle."

Her last request before her conversation with Caleb had been terminated was for him not to mention Mom and Dad's situation to her brothers. They were already paying their own way in life. Brigit wanted to do something on her own. For once.

Too bad it had cost her the love of her life.

"It's my mess," she said. "No one's cleaning it up but me."

She got off the phone with him but didn't go out to the main room. It was almost suppertime. She'd thrown a roast in the Crock-Pot—another way she was trying to contribute while she lived here. They could eat at any time, but then she'd witness "the looks." The tight glances between them and thinned lips because she wasn't laughing hard enough, or because she was listless, or because she really didn't look forward to spending the next who knew how many years under fluorescent lights, getting two fifteens and a thirty-minute break.

Though there was nowhere else to rush off to. She only needed to return to Moore to visit her family. There was no sexy rancher-slash-fireman waiting for her. Not anymore. Before, Caleb had underscored her reason for not returning. If it had been too hard to see him before, it would be heartbreaking now. Moore was too small, her family too tight, to not run across him. And with the way she'd been randomly breaking down into sobs, she wouldn't handle a run-in with him well.

She missed him.

She was so angry with him.

But...he was right. He'd waited all those years. Sure he'd dated, but he'd protected his heart and harbored enough hope to keep everyone else at a distance. But her? She'd run from one long-term relationship to another, convincing herself it was what she wanted.

A life with Caleb was what she wanted.

It was a fine mess she'd gotten herself into. Yet it wasn't anything less than she deserved. Her parents had given so much for all their kids, but Brigit had been the most selfish. And Caleb was free to live the life he deserved.

Tears welled, but she sniffled and blinked them back. It

was time for supper. She wasn't going to be very useful at work if she cried all night.

Trudging out to the kitchen, she avoided eye contact with her parents. Mom had just walked in and Dad was at the table, sorting through mail. Brigit started pulling out dishes. Her gaze fell on a tray of brownies from a bakery they'd gone to last week. The same place Brigit had lost her temper after one of her mom's censorious remarks. *I've gone without for ten years. I hope the next ten I can eat without guilt.*

Mom caught her looking. "You mentioned how much you liked them."

"Thanks." Mom had gone from food patrol to brownie pusher. *I only wanted to support your efforts to be healthy. I didn't realize you were so miserable.*

At least her time in Arizona had cleared up some misunderstandings between them.

Papers rustled at the table.

"What are these checks from Justin for?" Dad asked.

"He's selling the furniture you guys bought me." She loaded the plates on one arm and opened the cabinet with the glasses. "Another check should be arriving soon. I guess some stuff sold today. Then he'll work on selling the art."

Mom frowned and padded over to Dad. Her brow furrowed as she peered at the check. "Why is it made out to us? It's your furniture."

"You guys bought it. I'm gonna pay you back for that and for school."

"Brigit..." Mom sighed and scowled at the check. "Our decision to use our savings for you kids was our decision. You don't need to pay us back."

"I do, and I will." She set her armload on the table.

Mom's lips pursed. Brigit tensed, the familiar weight of Mom's perusal on her.

Mom shifted her gaze to Dad. "Put it aside for when

Brigit gets a new place, Rick." She stalked out of the kitchen, her shoulders rigid.

It wouldn't do to have them throw every cent back to her. "Dad, that money's not mine." Otherwise, she'd never prove that she could care for herself. "You guys paid for that furniture and it's not like I want to keep it after Oliver."

"Your mother's right. We have this figured out." The look he gave her was one of the most vulnerable she'd witnessed in her tough rancher dad. "I'll admit to being resistant to the idea of paying for as much school for you as we did for the boys. But I'd like to think I've updated with the times—and with your mom's not inconsiderable efforts. Three healthy kids with quality education? Three kids with the tools to do what they want in life? It was worth every cent. We wanted to help build your future. It's what parents do. We're proud of you." Dad cut his attention back to the mail. The conversation was over.

Dad didn't regret helping her through school. He was proud of her even though she could never pay him back. He wouldn't allow it.

If they weren't going to take something as simple as reimbursement for items they bought, how would she get them to accept part of her paychecks? And if she couldn't, then why the hell was she in Arizona in the first place?

Three kids with the tools to do what they want in life? She had the tools. All she needed was the courage.

THE CHATTER in the bar melted into a constant drone behind Caleb. He slumped over the one beer he was nursing. The Brigit story spilled out of him as Jesse and Farah listened. It wasn't easy sitting across from them. A couple that wasn't supposed to be, yet they were tighter and happier than ever.

Their wedding was scheduled for the one-year anniversary of the day the tornado had struck.

They'd asked him if he was okay with it, since that day was also the anniversary of his house being flung across the county. But he'd reassured them he'd rather have a happier time to remember on every anniversary anyway, and his new house should be underway by then.

Should be. He was settled into his new position and could handle a higher mortgage. A meeting with the banker and the home builder was tomorrow. He should be ecstatic. It was March. They could break ground in May and he could be in his new house in September. But they were nothing but items to check off like he would at the grocery store.

"I…" Farah chewed on her bottom lip and considered him.

"Go ahead and say whatever you don't want to say." It wasn't like he could hurt any more than he did now.

"Okay. I'm really surprised you aren't in Arizona right now."

Jesse nodded.

Caleb looked at them both. "I don't want to live in fucking Arizona."

Farah leaned across the table. "But Brigit's in Arizona. And she wants to be with you. Which, coincidentally, has been exactly what you've wanted ever since I've known you."

That was a long time. No one knew better than him. "She doesn't want me after what I said."

Jesse snorted. "It's called forgiveness. I'm living proof of how forgiving the Walkers can be. Seriously, though. Why did you stay here?"

"I just told you. I'm done being an afterthought for the women in my life." He glanced at Farah. "Present company excluded."

"I didn't give birth to you and I'm not the one you've

wanted for forever." She shook her head. "Can you really move on and be happy on your ranch? Going to work every day? Finding someone else?" She cocked a light brow at him.

The idea of finding someone else soured his stomach. Waking up alone after experiencing a few months of being with Brigit was propelling him toward insanity. Every morning, he'd open his eyes and stare at the ceiling and wonder if his pride was really that important. Had he thrown away his future to patch over his ego?

He didn't know. Had he hoped that telling Farah and Jesse what had happened would reinforce his decision? Because that was backfiring.

Farah broke into his thoughts. "I'm surprised that Brigit would pay them back. I guess I always thought of her as the pampered princess of that family. And yeah, she is. I get why it would be hard for her to walk away from the life track she had planned out, but to do it because she found out her parents drained their retirement for her school? I mean...a selfish person wouldn't do that."

Caleb took another swig of his lukewarm beer. "It feels more like a convenient excuse not to go through with shattering their expectations of her. In the Cities, she didn't even want to do anything. She claimed she wanted to come home."

"I get that," Jesse said. "I don't want to go back to living in a town bigger than Moore, either. St. Cloud, St. Paul, I don't care. Those places aren't my scene. Moore is my home."

Caleb leveled him with a stare. "But you'd still vacation there."

Jesse bobbed his head, the bar lights gleaming off his dark hair. "Hell, yeah. I'd get away with Farah anywhere. But Brigit was there for a job interview she didn't want."

"And wasn't it storming across the state?" Farah asked. "Isn't that why you went early in the first place?"

"It was still a mini vacation," he grumbled. The other two

stared at him, their expressions saying *sure it was*. "You two aren't helping."

"We're not helping with the pity party?" Farah asked. "Or we're not helping build an image of a selfish, vindictive girl who would end up treating you like your mom, which we all know is bullshit?"

"I didn't say *exactly* like my mom." He sighed and pinched the bridge of his nose. Perhaps Brigit's call had been nothing more than bad timing. He'd been at an emotional low and she'd… asked him to wait for her.

Fuck, how long had he wanted her to want him? And he'd pushed her away.

"I've gotta go." Caleb paused before he got up. "But thanks for the talk. I mean it."

He hoped they didn't think he was brushing them off and walking out in a huff, but he didn't wait around to see. He had emails to send.

On the way to Justin's, he formulated his plans. Once he was settled in his room, he pulled up his email. The home builder got a message first, canceling the meeting. The next email was for the banker, spelling out what he wanted to do instead.

Sleep was restless, but he powered through the waking-up-alone part. He was a man on a mission.

He flew through his chores, then dusted himself off and drove to town, grateful for all that money he'd spent keeping his good truck running. Swinging into the bank's parking lot, he found a spot. If it were any other banker, he probably would've gone home to change. But Dennis Gleason had worked with his family for years. Grandpa had sung the man's praises, that he'd kept them from rolling under several times.

"Caleb," Dennis greeted. "Come in."

Caleb selected a chair across from the expansive desk.

Pictures of Dennis's kids and grandkids lined the walls and bookshelves. Even artwork from one of his grandkids hung behind his chair. Dennis was family man. He'd know how big of a decision this was for Caleb.

"I was quite surprised by your email." Dennis sifted through some papers. "It's a sudden shift to go from building a home to selling the entire ranch."

"I assure you, it's not a decision I made lightly." Only impulsively.

"No, I can imagine." A line formed across Dennis's brow as he studied the forms in front of him. "I went back and pulled the information from the time your grandpa thought of selling."

"Excuse me?" This was news to him. His grandparents had died in that place. They'd wanted to sell?

"Yeah. Gosh, it was years ago. You were a teenager. But we started the process. I have all the appraisals from then. They'll be different now. Higher. Anyway." Dennis pushed the forms across the desk. "They decided not to when you planned to stay in Moore. Keeping the ranch limping along wasn't easy, but they wanted you to have something to your name, and a home if you ever needed it."

He had needed it.

His grandparents had kept the place for him? They'd continued ranching *for him* when they could've sold and, hell, moved to motherfucking Arizona? Dennis was right. They *had* limped along. He'd taken what Grandpa had taught him and wasn't doing much better. It was part of why his impulsive decision had made sense.

Now selling the ranch and chasing Brigit to Arizona was suddenly so complicated. So terribly complicated.

He was in possession of this very thing—a huge and major thing with a lot of cattle roaming on it—because his grandparents had worked and sacrificed for him.

How could he sell now that he knew that? They'd toiled for extra years, given up retirement, all so he could have more.

His chest burned as conflict raged inside. Was this what Brigit was feeling? So damn torn between everything her family had done for her and her own personal wants, which weren't trivial but seemed so compared to all that had been given up for her?

Fuck.

But he wasn't one to give up. "Dennis, I'll get back to you."

He was going to have to change his plans. He wasn't leaving, and she wasn't staying? Well, he could change that.

CHAPTER 17

"I hate all of this." Brigit studied her parents' reactions. Mom blinked at the sudden announcement. Dad folded his hands in front of himself. Call her a coward, but she'd waited until she had a ticket in hand and all her clothing packed before making her announcement.

It wasn't like Mom or Dad would jump in her way, or unload her items as she stuffed them in, or refuse to give her a ride to the airport. But Brigit wasn't working within her normal confines of being the good girl.

She continued. "The only good thing about this misadventure is that I got to hang out with you guys. But this isn't me." She slowly inhaled, lining steel up and down her spine. "I don't know how I'll ever repay you"—since they wouldn't accept her money—"but it won't be by living a life that I can't stand. I gave up Caleb *twice*. Once because I thought it was what I wanted, and who knows, maybe that was true then." But she was a stronger person now. "The second time because I thought I had to."

Mom looked away, guilt reflecting in her features. Dad's

expression grew grimmer the longer she talked. And she wasn't done talking.

"I'm not this girl. Growing up, I lived for racing through the pastures, but somewhere along the line, I convinced myself that kind of life wasn't for me as an adult. Even though adult me sees my siblings and my cousins doing it. I don't want a desk job. I want to use my education and expertise to help farmers and ranchers improve their processes and I want to continue building my expertise by doing it. I'm good at it."

Mom cocked her head, but her look wasn't challenging. "How?"

"I don't know. I'll apply to the Walker Five, or I'll find someone who needs a hired hand and doesn't balk at boobs. But the first thing I'm going to do is talk to Caleb." Could she patch the rift between them? Her anger had faded, replaced by understanding. He was owed one outburst after ten years. He'd had so many reasons to tell her to fuck off, so she shouldn't be startled when he finally had. "He makes me feel good about myself. I have fun with him. Real fun. That may sound insignificant, but I've been miserable for years. And I wouldn't have been if I'd opened up and talked to Caleb and you two in the first place. But thanks to him, I'm comfortable enough with myself to do that now."

He'd done so much for her. The unshakable Caleb had been hurt one too many times, and she'd been one of the ones wielding a knife.

Would he take her back?

"My flight leaves soon, and I need to get to the airport." Both her parents' brows shot up. "Sorry for the short notice." She'd pondered this move for days. When she'd gotten her first paycheck and her parents had turned down her money, she'd booked a flight and started packing, then drafted her immediate resignation as a market research analyst.

Dad cleared his throat. "Do you need a ride?"

She nodded.

Mom and Dad's muffled words followed her out of the room as she retrieved her luggage. Only one more suitcase than she'd come with. Not bad. The new business clothing she'd bought wouldn't do much good cleaning barns or helping with lambing and calving. They wouldn't even be good for the ranching workshops she'd drafted in her head during her breaks and lunches. But these two suitcases were all she had to her name.

The ride to the airport was quiet. A million times, she wanted to ask Mom if she was okay, or what she thought, but Brigit refrained. She was leaving. Mom would talk when she was ready. Perhaps she just needed time. The closer they got to the airport, the more Mom's silence bothered her.

Were the two scenarios compatible? Could she have a tight-knit relationship with her mother and be with Caleb too? If Caleb even took her back. She hadn't given him much reason to.

The quick hugs at the terminal were awkward and cold. Mom's eyes shone, and she was as stiff as taffy in winter. Brigit held her own tears back as Mom barely looked at her. Dad gave her a reassuring smile.

"I'll call Justin," he offered. "I imagine you haven't told him…about us?"

Brigit shook her head.

"Yeah." His blue eyes turned sad. "You're awfully good at keeping everything close to the vest."

Shame washed over her. She'd hurt them. All those years of trying to be a daughter they could be proud of had only created a wide expanse between them.

"I'm sorry" was all she could say.

"We'll talk later. I'll let Justin know when to pick you up. And if he can't, well… I guess I should call Travis anyway."

"Thank you."

Mom was already in the car, staring straight ahead. Dad nodded and went around to get inside. Brigit looked at the bustle of people getting out of cabs and Ubers and dragging their bags to the sidewalk. She sighed and followed their lead, going through the actions of check-in and security, her mind bouncing from what-if to what-if.

The flight had no delays. As they approached her small hometown airport, nerves fluttered in her belly, growing in strength the closer the ground got. She pressed her fingers to her lips.

She was coming back home. Again with no job, no support, and all alone. Again asking her brother to save her. Again she'd move in next to Caleb and— Oh God, what if he didn't want to listen to her? What if he was done with her? What if he realized that he was so much better off without her?

The plane bumped as it touched down. She impatiently shuffled through the aisle behind the few other people coming back to Moore. At least her timing with one thing in life had worked out. She'd gotten the last flight to Moore before they shut down airbus service to Phoenix. Flights would start up again in November, when people fled the winter to get back to the land of the sun.

Justin waited for her inside the small airport, behind the large glass window that overlooked the runway. His features were haggard. His once carefully trimmed hair stuck out from under the brim of his hat. He had his hands stuck in the pockets of his North Face parka and he silently watched her approach.

She mustered a smile. "Hey, thanks for picking me up."

"Yeah." He dragged the word out. "When Dad called and asked if I had time to talk and told me why, I said I might as well stay here and hear him out. You know, since I was already here to drop Caleb off."

Caleb was flying somewhere? Had he ever been on a plane?"

"Yep. Your phone must've been off by the time we tried to call you. Caleb is probably landing in Arizona as we speak."

❧

WITH HIS SMALL carry-on duffel bag, Caleb strode out the doors of the airport into temperatures that wouldn't hit Moore until June. His hooded sweatshirt and cowboy boots were almost too warm, but it was a nice change from freezing weather. No wonder people escaped to Arizona each winter.

He doubted any of them had the same reason he did.

His first flight was uneventful. Jesse had agreed to watch the ranch for an indefinite amount of time. His boss had scowled and said he wasn't going to fill the position until Caleb was one hundred percent, absolutely, positively sure he was moving to Arizona. He had no idea if Brigit would slam the door in his face, but he didn't have to worry about that yet. He was armed with Rick and Joan's address and planned to find a good old-fashioned taxi. Justin had described the layout of the airport, told him exactly which door to exit from, and how to find a ride.

He scanned for the signs Justin had described as he'd given him a ride to the airport.

"Caleb."

The voice was familiar, but who the hell would he know at the Phoenix airport? He spun around. Rick Walker stood only feet away in chinos and a short-sleeved button-up shirt.

"Rick?" He couldn't keep the surprise out of his voice. In

Moore, running across Rick would've been a coincidence. In a city with like two million people? No. "Is everything okay?"

The man looked tired. His graying blond hair was disheveled, and his shoulders hung like a ton of weight had been dumped on them. "I think it might be. But if you're looking for Brigit, you won't find her here."

Ice collected in Caleb's veins. Rick Walker was intercepting him at the airport to keep him away from Brigit? At her request? Had Justin called ahead?

But just as his brain reached maximum panic, Rick said, "She's in Moore."

Caleb stared at the guy. "Who's in Moore? Brigit?" His mind couldn't reconcile the information.

"Justin's picking her up. When we called, he told us you were rushing here for her." Rick shrugged, his expression lightening back to the laid-back dad Caleb had known. "I guess you each were so intent on getting to the other. Maybe one of you should've called first."

"I...didn't know if she'd answer." And he'd wanted his surprise to prove how committed he was. Long-distance cr selling the ranch and moving here—he'd do it. As long as she still wanted to be with him.

"She must've thought the same. Or maybe it didn't matter. She quit her job and moved out."

"She did what now?" Brigit quit to move *back* to Moore? For him? He didn't dare hope.

"Did you know she only took a job out here because she thought she had to pay us back?"

He nodded.

"But you knew how much she wanted to go into the family business?"

He nodded again. "She wanted to be a part of it, not just a worker bee."

The weight dropped back on Rick's shoulders. "That's all she would've been too. Her mother was right. But now will be different. Brigit will make sure of it." He sighed and straightened. "There are no more direct flights to Moore until next season. Why don't you come back to our place, get a bite to eat, and we'll book a flight back. We need to talk anyway."

Caleb tried to process the abrupt change in plans on the way to Rick's car. For his part, Rick rattled on about Phoenix on the way to his house. Caleb dipped his head occasionally to let the guy know he was listening, even if he wasn't paying attention. The architecture, the difference in weather, and factoids about the neighborhoods they were driving through were of little interest to him.

Brigit had flown back to Moore. She'd obviously talked to her parents. She'd quit her job and gone home to do what she wanted. Yet, Rick made it sound like she'd gone back for him.

Too soon, Rick pulled into the garage of a reddish-tan stucco house that looked like every other house on the block. So different from the older homes of Moore, and all in a style he'd never seen outside of TV until now. It would be fascinating if his mind didn't keep returning to Brigit.

Joan was here. Rick had never intimidated him, and he'd always been friendly and congenial, asking about his grandparents and the ranch. Sometimes they'd joke around, but Rick had always been busy with his own work, and Caleb and Justin had been up to their own shenanigans.

Joan, though.

Acid roiled in his stomach. Was she the one who'd deliver the "stay away from my daughter" talk? How would he deal with that? What happened between him and Brigit was their business only, but her mom was important to her. He didn't have to have a close relationship with his own to understand.

If anything, he understood the importance of that relationship *because* he didn't have one of his own.

Rick led him inside, waving off his attempt to take his boots off. "We always wear our shoes here. The floor's too hard not to."

Caleb's boots clicked on the floor, echoing off the walls. He passed frames of Brigit and her brothers. Photos of Travis and Kami, and even more of their kids—school pictures of Kambria and baby photos of Ben. Turning into the kitchen, he spotted Joan. Her eyes were red and puffy, and she had a mug of steaming tea between her hands.

When she looked at him, her eyes were haunted. "Have a seat, Caleb."

A plate waited for him at the table, in a spot between her and where Rick was settling in.

God this was uncomfortable.

A muffin rested on the plate. If he tried to eat it now, it'd turn to dust in his dry mouth.

As his butt hit the hard chair, he realized this was the first time Joan had set a place at the table for him. Growing up, it was always, "Oh, I thought your mom was picking you up." He and Justin had cruised through the kitchen whenever they'd wanted, grabbing food as they went, but when it came to meal times, Caleb was not part of the family.

Joan sniffed and raised her watery gaze to him. "I've been awful to you."

Caleb laid his clammy hands on his jeans. Had he heard correctly? Did he agree like a bastard kicking her while she down? Or did he continue this farce by politely demurring?

Joan's gaze switched to her mug. The tea bag floated inside. Had she even taken a sip? "I didn't realize how private Brigit was until today. But it's all in what she doesn't say, isn't it?" Her chuckle was as dry as the rocky landscape outside.

"Oliver was insulting and degrading. It was subtle, and she hardly mentioned it at the time. It's why we helped buy all that furniture. But we thought she was in love."

"She thought she was in love," Rick added. "I think that was the problem with all those guys. She thought she should be in love with them."

Joan nodded, her expression sage. "I can't help but wonder if she stayed with him so long because she thought I liked him. As if I'd approve of a man who made my daughter feel horrible."

Caleb's brow rose of its own accord, but Joan saw before he could correct it.

She huffed, but it wasn't aimed at him. "I know, right? Apparently, *I've* been making her feel horrible."

He dipped his head. Joan was in a no-bullshit mood.

"The older she got, the more insecure she became. I thought I was helping her, not reinforcing those insecurities. I thought I was the support she needed. Those relationships seemed like what she really wanted, and I encouraged them." Tears welled, and she inhaled a shaky breath. "She never said otherwise. You want to know what else she didn't say?"

He kept his mouth shut. He had no idea where Joan was going with this, but this was the most she'd said to him in his entire life.

"She never said you treated her poorly. Because you didn't. Right?"

His voice cracked. "I would never." He hung his head. "Except for the last time I talked to her."

Joan adamantly shook her head. "You never made her feel bad about her looks, her height, or her weight. You never made her search for a career she hated to make you happy. You never..." Joan's direct gaze tagged his. "You never held me against her."

"I…" Well, they were being honest. "I have always loved her."

"And I knew that. I could see how you adored her." Joan reached across the table, her hand stretching out. He brought one hand up, unsure of what to do. Joan gripped him, her fingers curled around his. "All this time, you were the one smoothing the way for her to be herself. And I held your upbringing against you."

He stiffened at the mention of his past, but Joan squeezed his hand. "For what it's worth, my comments were aimed at your mother. But the target they hit was you. I should've kept my mouth shut and supported you."

Rick scooted closer and patted his shoulder. This moment was more affection than what his own parents had shown him.

"I can be overly protective of my children," she continued. "And the way I go about it has hurt others. I justified it to myself, thinking that you had so much stacked against you, you'd only drag Brigit down."

He flinched. It was one thing to suspect it, but to hear it was another.

"I did the same thing with Travis's wife." Her words were barely audible. "It scares me to think of how I could've interfered with his happiness. I think it's time I learned my lesson."

"We're awfully proud of you, Caleb," Rick said gruffly. "You were a good kid, a little reckless, but the man you grew up to be would make any parent proud."

Caleb snorted. "Not any parent."

"I'm sorry," Joan whispered. "You've faced more than I can ever know. Justin tells us about you. Finishing school. Your recent promotion. The way you help him and still run your ranch."

"I have a lot of help." He couldn't take all the credit when Justin, Jesse, and Farah backed him up.

"As you should." Rick sat back in his chair. "I had four brothers and it was a hard life. Selling cars is a whole lot easier than selling cows."

Joan patted his hand and sat back. "But it's what Brigit wants. She told me about the extra courses she took. I think it doubled her guilt."

It had.

Rick nodded. "Joan and I are doing just fine. We put our kids through school like we wanted to, and we live in a nice home and enjoy our jobs. It was worth putting retirement off."

"It may take a while for Brigit to see that, but I think you can help. Here's what we're going to do."

Caleb braced himself, but never would he have guessed what they had planned.

BRIGIT DANCED from boot to boot. Her gloves and winter coat were heavy enough to ward off the chill. Her nose was probably pink, but she didn't care. Caleb would be walking out these doors at any moment.

The last few hours had been excruciating. Justin had brought her to the car that Brock had fixed up for her—a present from all the cousins, with a full tank of gas—then sent her off with the name of a hotel and a time of arrival.

It was quite a gamble, but Dad had texted that Caleb was on his way to Minneapolis. They'd flown Caleb there, and she could drive and get him—after they spent the night. The getaway was a little gift from her parents, paid for with furniture money.

Then Mom had called. The trip to the city had been full

of confessions and tears. Brigit was flayed and exposed, but so much lighter and more optimistic than she'd been when she'd woken up that morning.

She was peering at all the passersby—as if she could ever miss Caleb—when a solid wall of warmth plowed into her. A gasp ripped out of her as she was spun around. Before she could stare at his handsome face and marvel over the way his silky hair hung on his forehead and how much she wanted to run her hands through it, he enveloped her in a tight hug.

"Oh my God, I missed you," he breathed into her neck.

She wrapped her arms around him, wishing she'd ditched the coat in her car so she could be closer to him. "I'm so sorry."

"No, I'm the one who's sorry."

"No—" But any more argument died on her lips as he smashed his mouth against hers.

Minutes ticked by, but she had no wish to detach herself from him. A guy walked by muttering, "Get a room."

She pulled away and gazed up at him. "We have one."

"One what?" His pupils were wide and his gaze hot.

"A room."

"Right. Your mom mentioned that."

She nodded, still lined up with him, her arms around his neck. "She said she talked to you."

"It was the most surreal moment of my life. I'm not convinced it really happened."

She giggled. "It did. They covered your flight. Justin got the room. And you can call your boss and tell him you'll be at your next shift." Tracing her finger down his cheek, she could barely talk. "I can't believe you were going to sell your place and quit your job to come to Arizona."

"I would've." He turned his head to kiss her palm. "Where's your car? We're going to need that room."

She pulled him with her, giving him only enough time to grab his bag.

"I hope we don't have to go far." His low growl sent tingles coursing down her back.

She wanted to get to the room as badly as he did. She pointed to the tall building to their left. "It'll only take a couple of minutes. Justin seemed to think we wouldn't want to drive far, and I had time to check in before I came here."

In the time it took to drive to the hotel, Caleb told her about the fallout with his mom and what he'd learned at the bank. "I realized the bad position you were in," he confessed.

"I put myself in it. You didn't." She parked, and they wasted zero seconds getting up to the room.

Her hands were shaking as she swiped the key card. It refused to work. Caleb finally snatched the card, got them inside, and kicked the door closed behind him. Just like the last time they were in a hotel room, he crowded her against the wall, but he didn't move as fast. Instead, he cupped her face and kissed her lips once, then twice.

"I'm so in love with you," he murmured. "I can't believe I almost messed it up."

"I've always been in love with you, and I messed it up for so many years." She laid her hands on his chest, needing to reassure herself that he was here with her.

"Yet, here we are. If we can't keep ourselves apart, nothing else will." He caught her mouth in a soft kiss that grew harder. Needier.

She gripped his sweatshirt and yanked up. They broke apart only to strip each other down, but he didn't take her against the wall.

He stepped back, his shaft so rigid it didn't even bob with his movement.

"You're so damn beautiful."

He made her feel that way. Taking her hand, he tugged her to him and swept her into his arms.

She managed to keep the volume down on her squeal. "You give me a heart attack when you do that."

He grinned, but it faded quickly. Desire washed out everything else in his eyes. "I need to be in you now."

"Yes."

He set her on the bed and covered her with his body. Nudging her legs part with his knee, he dropped his head to hers, licking his tongue along the seam of her mouth. She opened for him and spread her legs. There was no need for foreplay, no reason to wait.

Maybe one. "You're still on the pill."

"Yes, and no, we don't need a condom." Whatever happened now would be at the right time and it'd be with Caleb.

Dragging the head of his cock through her wetness, he paused only to position himself before he thrust inside. Her ragged gasp mingled with his raw groan. He thrust and stilled, and their gazes clashed. He took his time withdrawing and slamming in. Lifting her pelvis, she gave him as much access as she could. He rose to his arms, a slight quiver traveling through his body.

"I need…" He panted and rocked his hips. "I wanted to wait, but I want to marry you. I want a life with you. My ranch is your ranch and I want you at my side when we plan our home together."

His arms shook as he strained to hold still. His coiled power between her legs was intoxicating and made it nearly impossible not to undulate under him, to stroke herself along his length.

"Yes, Caleb. I will marry you."

A slow grin spread across his face. "Say it again." He bucked his hips.

The burst of ecstasy robbed her of air, but she forced the words out. "Yes, Caleb, I will marry you."

He lost himself and she went with him, each straining with the other, rapture building, until he threw his head back, his teeth clenched. Her body tightened as her orgasm hit. She clamped around him, milking his release. She wanted it all. To share his name, his home, his babies, his ranch. Her life was finally her own, and she chose to be with him.

As Brigit pulled the pickup into the parking lot of the farm and supply store, the inset diamond on her engagement ring winked in the light. The band was perfect and simple, and while she'd have to take it off to go shoulder-deep into the back end of a cow, she didn't otherwise have to worry about it hindering her work. She'd insisted she didn't need one, but Caleb was stubborn that way and had surprised her with a ring that was perfect for her.

They hadn't gotten out of bed for hours after he'd presented her with it. That was two months ago.

She parked. It was the middle of August and she'd used the pickup more than Caleb, since she was running the ranch. He often drove the car Brock had given her—a cheap buy at a car auction that he refused to let her pay him back for. But she didn't feel guilty. As much knowledge and experience as her cousins had running their operation, they'd consulted her several times, and not just for show. She was their personal consultant and she charged them nothing—because she was finally in a place to give back.

Plus, she offered free babysitting for all of them and none

had failed to take her up on it. Caleb had the time of his life watching kids and they spent much of their time reminiscing about when they were younger. Then talk turned to starting their own family, but since their wedding was this weekend, neither was in a hurry to get started expanding. She wanted to oversee one calving season before she dealt with her own pregnancy status.

Caleb pointed to another familiar truck. "There's Justin. He's already here with your parents."

"Great. They'll just come home with us." Justin had gotten them from the airport so she and Caleb could run a few more last-minute wedding errands. Mom and Dad would stay at their place for the night, but after the wedding, they'd be with Justin.

They wanted the full experience of the new house Caleb and Brigit had moved into a week ago. The place was done a month early. Unprecedented, the builder had said, but it wasn't like she and Caleb could afford all the extras. It was still a nice two-story ranch home. The design was similar to the previous house, but a century more updated.

She climbed out. Caleb hooked his arm around her shoulders and they walked in. Teddy smiled and waved at her. She'd made sure there were no repeats of that first time, and she'd done the same at the auto parts store and the repair garage she took projects to that she couldn't fix herself—and only if Jesse was too busy to be hired out.

Thanks to Farah, Brigit had a best friend she could talk to about both wedding plans and calving rates.

When she spotted her parents chatting with someone concealed behind a tower display of watering cans, she changed direction, Caleb moving with her.

She leaned over to whisper to Caleb. "Farah's coming over to help make the birdseed sachets Mom insisted on."

She would've been fine with a small wedding, or even a

courthouse wedding, but she'd told Caleb that she didn't want to fly under the radar marrying him. She wanted the world to know. It was going to happen, even on a budget. And birdseed was cheap enough.

Caleb snorted. "I'd say something like 'I can't wait to get a load of you two getting all crafty,' but I know my ass is going to be stuck beside you getting them ready."

Her laughter drew the attention of customers. The man her parents chatted up leaned around the watering cans.

"Look at that," Brigit said under her breath. It was Oliver. He was dressed in what he usually wore to the office.

"Oh, Brigit. Caleb." Mom stretched her arms out, and she wasn't putting on a show. Mom loved Caleb, and while Caleb might have tried to maintain some distance out of fear of rejection, it hadn't lasted long. He talked on the phone more to Mom than she did.

"Mama." Caleb hugged her, lifting her feet off the ground.

"Oliver," Brigit greeted coolly before shifting her attention to her dad. "How was the flight?"

"Can't wait for the straight shot to open up again." Dad shook his head. "I can do without the cardio racing to the opposite end of the Minneapolis airport for the second leg."

Mom gave her a quick hug and stepped back. "I was just telling Oliver how exciting it is to add another son to our brood." She playfully elbowed Caleb. "And a local hero at that."

Caleb had driven his fire engine—apparatus, if she could ever get used to calling it that—in the local Fourth of July parade. Mom and Dad had made sure to come back for it. The parade was typically a family affair with Travis and her cousins driving their tractors and Kambria riding horse for 4H, so Caleb had been the icing on the cake.

Oliver's gaze swept her body. She had never dressed like this when she was with him—a simple T-shirt and dusty jeans with her cowboy boots. Her hair was in a ponytail and she had her Walker Five hat on. Caleb liked how it brought out the yellow in her eyes.

"Uh, congratulations on the wedding." His eyes dipped to her breasts again and the male interest was clear. He caught Caleb's steady stare, swallowed hard, and looked away.

Oliver liked how she looked? So all those pointed comments about her weight and her ass had just been about control? She'd known that, but still. What an ass.

"Thank you." She'd never been the type to whip out the perfect catty comment. Now would be an ideal time, but she had no more energy to waste on Oliver.

"So, what are you doing now?" he asked. She tensed. She knew that tone. A mixture of smug and fake curiosity.

"I run Circle Cruise Cattle Ranch and give workshops on financing in the industry and new trends. In my downtime, I write freelance articles for magazines." Her downtime in the winter, but she didn't add that yet.

Oliver covered his surprise with the faint sneer she knew too well.

"And," she continued, "the best part is that the only bullshit I have to deal with anymore is from the cattle." Look at that. The perfect catty comment, thanks to no longer caring what he thought.

Caleb tried to cover his laugh with a cough, but her parents didn't bother. Oliver pivoted on his heel and stalked away.

"Solid burn," Caleb said.

Mom clapped her hands together. "Now that the ass has been dealt with, let's get to wedding festivities."

Mom cupped Dad's elbow and dragged him along. Caleb's arm remained around her shoulder. She twined her fingers through his. As they rounded a corner, they had to sidestep an older woman.

The lady smiled at them and gestured to their interlocked fingers. "Oh my heart. Seeing couples like you makes my day."

The barista's words from nearly a year ago ran through her mind. *"I just love seeing couples so into each other. And when the man dotes on his woman like that..."*

"Thank you," Brigit said. "He's all mine."

ARE CALEB AND BRIGIT RIGHT: Should Justin have fallen for Priya? Is it too late? Find out in White Collar Rancher.

I'D LOVE to hear what you thought. You can drop a quick review of Red Hot Rancher at the retailer.

FOR ALL THE LATEST NEWS, sneak peeks, quarterly short stories, and free material sign up for my newsletter.

ABOUT THE AUTHOR

Marie Johnston writes paranormal and contemporary romance and has collected several awards in both genres. Before she was a writer, she was a microbiologist. Depending on the situation, she can be oddly unconcerned about germs or weirdly phobic. She's also a licensed medical technician and has worked as a public health microbiologist and as a lab tech in hospital and clinic labs. Marie's been a volunteer EMT, a college instructor, a security guard, a phlebotomist, a hotel clerk, and a coffee pourer in a bingo hall. All fodder for a writer!! She's married with four kids.

mariejohnstonwriter.com
Facebook
Twitter @mjohnstonwriter
Instagram @mariejohnstonwriter

ALSO BY MARIE JOHNSTON

Part-Time Cowboys
Rancher in Training (Book 1)
Red Hot Rancher (Book 2)
White Collar Rancher (Book 3)
Rancher Next Door (Book 4)
Her Christmas Offer (novella)